Praise for *The*

'A masterwork of historical ficti
American prairie'

'A clear-eyed and riveting account of one womans journey into
a so-called land of opportunity . . . Sarah is a powerful narrator,
utterly devoid of self-pity, a woman who observes herself and
others with ruthless honesty'   *Guardian*

'In replacing long-held legends with historic traumas, Moore's
steely vision of the American west recognizes few, if any, heroes.
The result is a repudiation – solemn yet stirring – of the ideal-
ized fable of the American West'   *Washington Post*

'I find Moore to be one of the most compelling novelists alive.
The Lost Wife is concise and brutally incisive. As ever, Susanna
Moore is unflinching'   Stephanie Danler, author of *Sweetbitter*

'Impressively taut and evocative . . . A captivating period piece
that brings life on the frontier into vivid, often brutal focus
through the prism of female experience . . . Although at first
glance, *The Lost Wife* appears to be very different to Moore's
most famous work, her erotically-charged thriller *In the Cut*,
both novels are intimately concerned with sex, violence and
language'   *Telegraph*

'A compelling tale of survival, loyalty and exploitation'
                                                          The Bookseller

'Based partly on a woman's account of her abduction along with
her children during the Sioux Uprising in 1862, Moore's novel
is a tense, absorbing tale of adversity and survival . . . Moore
has imagined a brave, perceptive woman with no illusions about
the hypocrisy of those who proclaim themselves civilized . . . A
devastating tale rendered with restrained serenity'
                                          Kirkus Reviews, starred review

The Lost Wife

The Lost Will

The Lost Wife

SUSANNA MOORE

WEIDENFELD & NICOLSON

First published in the United States in 2023 by Alfred A. Knopf,
First published in Great Britain in 2023 by Weidenfeld & Nicolson,
This paperback edition published in 2024 by Weidenfeld & Nicolson,
an imprint of The Orion Publishing Group Ltd
Carmelite House, 50 Victoria Embankment
London EC4Y 0DZ

An Hachette UK Company

3 5 7 9 10 8 6 4

A CIP catalogue record for this book is
available from the British Library.

ISBN (Mass Market Paperback) 978 1 3996 1254 8
ISBN (eBook) 978 1 3996 1255 5
ISBN (Audio) 978 1 3996 1256 2

Printed in Great Britain by Clays Ltd, Elcograf, S.p.A.

MIX
Paper from
responsible sources
FSC® C104740

www.weidenfeldandnicolson.co.uk
www.orionbooks.co.uk

For Jasper

Susanna Moore is the author of the novels *The Life of Objects*, *The Big Girls*, *One Last Look*, *In the Cut*, *Sleeping Beauties*, *The Whiteness of Bones* and *My Old Sweetheart*, and three books of non-fiction, *Light Years: A Girlhood in Hawai'i*, *I Myself Have Seen It: The Myth of Hawai'i* and *Miss Aluminium*. She lives in New York City.

The Lost Wife

June 1855

I PRETENDED TO BE ASLEEP until Ank left the room. Florence was with Ank's sister Viola in Kingstown, and the house was quiet. When I could hear Ank in the shop, I jumped from bed and dressed, stuffing two books, a penknife, a dress, a salami, a moth-eaten tartan cape, and Maddie's letters into a cardboard suitcase. The letters are two years old, but I have read them so many times, I know every word by heart. She says there is work to be had in the West, not just saloon-girl work like in the penny weeklies, but work you wouldn't be ashamed to do. I wonder if she will be surprised to see me. Surprised to see I am alone. She never believed I would do it. I counted the money I'd saved, which came to forty-two dollars. I kept thirty dollars for myself and wrapped the rest in a piece of butcher's paper, sealed it in an envelope, and addressed it.

When I heard Mr. Lombardi in the alley, I invited him into the kitchen for coffee. He delivers a supply of colored glass stones to the shop on the last Monday of the month, and I was expecting him. I told him I needed to get to Boston, where my sister was ill. I have no sister, but he did not know that. If he would take me to the Fox Point station when he left, I could catch the afternoon train to Boston. When he agreed, I asked him not to tell Ank. I said I had been forbidden to see my sister, as she lived in sin with another woman. It was the worst lie I could devise.

My wrist is bandaged where my husband burned me with the soldering flame, and I saw Mr. Lombardi glance at it, but he said nothing. He knew Ank did it. Everyone in our street knows Ank likes to hurt me. Viola knows. My mother knew, although she never did anything to stop it. "It is only what you deserve," she said. "Anyone with the name Aniketos cannot be a proper Christian and has to be a foreigner, maybe even a Greek. Or worse, a Turk." How she determined that Greeks are not Christians is a mystery, but there is a long list of mysteries where my mother is concerned. Who, for instance, is my father? She refused to tell me. Maybe he, too, is Greek, which would account for my black eyes and hair, and the faint line of fuzz above my lip. She believed that during conception, the partner who had the strongest orgasm determined the looks of the child, which suggests that my father is Greek after all. Or a Turk. And that she is as cold as ice, but I knew that.

I met Mr. Lombardi on Eddy Street as we had planned. It was raining and we were soon wet through, despite the tarp he threw over us. He had a pint of whiskey in his pocket and now and then took a drink, but he did not offer me any. He dropped me at the Fox Point station, and I again reminded him that he was not to tell anyone he had seen me. When he handed down my suitcase, he slipped a half-dollar into my hand, which caused me to wonder if he believed my story after all. As I watched him turn the corner, I told myself that everything that happened from then on would be a sign. Even the rain was a sign. It would erase my footprints.

I mailed the envelope and ran into the station. I arrived too late to catch the train to Albany and spent the night in the waiting room. I thought the porters who wandered in and out might not like it if I sat on one of their benches in wet clothes, so I walked in circles to keep warm, eating the salami and shaking with cold. Every time a man came through the door, I was certain it was Ank and hid my face in my sleeve, but no one bothered me, except for one man who asked if I was free for the evening.

I read Maddie's instructions for the hundredth time. Once I reach Albany, I will board an Erie Canal packet boat which will get me as far as Buffalo. In Buffalo, I am to take a lake steamer to Chicago. The fare in steerage will be three dollars. In Chicago, I am to find a place on a wagon traveling to a port on the Mississippi River called Galena. Then another steamboat from Galena to the town of Shakopee, Minnesota, where Maddie will be waiting for me.

. . .

I must have fallen asleep on the train to Albany, as I don't remember leaving Boston. I was nudged awake by the conductor, surprised to see wheat fields and cows and barns. I asked if he knew how I might find the Erie Canal Navigation Company in Albany, which he said was a fifteen-minute walk from the station.

I made my way there as soon as we arrived and bought a ticket on what is called a line boat, departing in an hour. It is sixty feet long and ten feet wide, and used mainly for freight, which, the clerk warned me, meant not as select a company as I would find on a packet boat. As it is drawn by mules rather than horses, it is slower, but it is also cheaper. I am paying one cent a mile, which comes to $3.90. It will take five days to reach Buffalo.

I used Mr. Lombardi's half-dollar to buy peanuts and a ham sandwich and a bottle of cider, reckoning it an unexpected treat, and ate the peanuts while I waited on the landing. Alongside me was an elderly woman holding a small gilded cage with a white rabbit in it. Also a minister who asked if he might preach to us from the Bible. I didn't know how I could refuse and said nothing, but the woman with the rabbit said, "I'd prefer not. I'm given to seizures."

. . .

It is my second day on the line boat. I sit on a three-legged stool on the roof of the main cabin. There are two spindly chairs in the bow, occupied by the old lady and her rabbit. Barrels and crates line each side of the boat. I sleep belowdecks on a sacking mattress. The others sleep on cots packed into the main cabin at night, the men separated from the women by a serge curtain strung on a sagging wire.

I feel unaccountably pleased with myself. I haven't felt this way in a long time, maybe never. I am on my way to Buffalo. No one has clapped his hands around my neck or burned me. Except for Mr. Lombardi, I haven't told a lie in days. Now and then, I am frightened by my freedom, wondering what I am meant to do with it. In the past, that is a week ago, it was a relief when things remained merely themselves.

One of the boatmen, a slight Irish boy, high-shouldered and bony with a chipped front tooth, saw that I had no dinner last night and told me that I could eat each evening in the main cabin, provided I pay for it. "It will cost you twenty cents," he said, taking a certain pride in what seemed to him an exorbitance. Tonight I sat at a long communal table with the boatmen and the old woman and ate baked beans and pork and green tomatoes. No one spoke, which was fine with me.

Later when I opened my suitcase, I saw that my penknife was missing.

.   .   .

The boy's name is Dennis. He told me he was an orphan with a sister in a convent in Ottawa, which did not surprise me as I'd learned at Dexter to spot an orphan a mile away. He has a tin whistle, a Doolin whistle, he says, and when the teasing by his fellow hands goes too far (the outline of a large crucifix is clearly visible beneath his shirt), he plays his whistle until they settle down. When he saw a book in my lap, he said he was teaching himself to read and asked if he could borrow it from me. I gave him *Ivanhoe*, as I had finished it that morning and did not wish to carry it. He returned half an hour later, having noticed it was a library book, to ask if he was breaking the law as the book was long overdue, but I assured him it would be all right. When my hat blew away, he gave me his neckerchief to wear around my head.

Last night, I dreamed that Florence and I lived in Nova Scotia, and this morning I almost jumped from the boat to find my way home, even though I know Ank would kill me.

. . .

I neglected to bring certain necessities in my haste, not only food, but the means to wash myself. When I began to bleed, I had nothing to put between my legs. Dennis must have seen the blood on my skirt, but he said nothing, handing me a few dirty dishcloths with the tips of his fingers, as if I had already soiled them. He sits on the deck beside my chair when we stop for the night to practice his letters on the endpapers of *Ivanhoe*. I suspect that he would like to visit me later, but I do not fancy him. Besides, although I am not what you would call fat, I would flatten him.

It is his job to shout "Bridge!" when we are about to pass under one, as there is often scant headroom. Those of us sitting on the flat roof, usually only myself and a stout man in a red wig, throw ourselves onto the deck until it is safe to regain our seats. Dennis was severely reprimanded yesterday when his warning came too late and a drunk drummer and his blind dog were knocked into the canal. Today I left the boat at one of its many stops to walk along the towpath, avoiding the mud and dung as best I could. At each landing, a boy appears with a broom to sweep the dung into the canal.

Men jump on and off the boat all day, mainly quarreling and laughing in a loud way as they load and unload goods, or to hitch a ride to the next landing. As we slowly move west, there are more languages, people speaking what I think is Swedish or German, and there is more noise, as if people's voices have to cover longer distances. There are more oxen and mules. More guns. More men than women. Ladies wear simple cloth sunbonnets, their skirts cut short to keep them from the dirt. A number of people are missing some part of themselves, eyes and whole rows of teeth and fingers and legs, and have added things, too, like glass eyes and hooks for hands. I saw a bargeman with shiny red streaks on his bald head, and I heard someone say he'd been scalped by Apaches in the Mexican war. That is the other thing. There are Indians.

. . .

One more day until we reach Buffalo. An elderly woman in mourning holding by the neck a boy with a black eye boarded the boat this morning, and a young clergyman who looked to be drunk. I saw him again, leaning against the railing at the stern of the boat, and I bid him good morning. His collar was stained with mud, and he smelled of piss. There was something false about him, not that priests do not drink or need a bath now and then. He seemed very pleased to be addressed. He said he was on his way to Niagara Falls, where he'd been appointed rector at a Methodist church. As I edged my way past him, he said, "Say, you couldn't loan me a buck, could you?" "No," I said, and he put out his foot and tripped me.

. . .

Maddie wrote that when I reached Buffalo, I was to find my way to the Steamboat Authority, and that is what I did. I paid three dollars for a place in steerage and was given a soiled pallet, a wooden stool, and a bucket without a handle. The clerk did not ask me my name. No one asked me my name.

It will take three days to reach Chicago. I bought a bag of plums, some pork rind, and a loaf of bread on the dock, but I finished them the second night. I'm hungry. I also smell bad. The boat is named *The Queen of the West*, and at night I can hear piano music and the stomping of feet and shouting as the passengers dance in the saloon above me.

During the day, I read *Villette* by Miss Charlotte Brontë. It is one of Maddie's favorite books and she recommended it, perhaps because I'd once told her I hoped to be a schoolteacher. I like it very much, especially as Lucy Snowe is plain like me, but it is hard to concentrate, and I am unable to read it as it deserves to be read. Besides, it is too dark to read at night.

. . .

The streets of Chicago are deep in mud, sometimes reaching as high as the bed of a wagon. The river is full of sewage and dead cows. I made my way to the shipping agency, slipping and sliding in the mud as I stopped to ask for directions. One man offered to take me there himself—it was only a few blocks away—if I would go with him to his room for five minutes. I didn't imagine he had a quick hand of gin in mind, but five minutes!

The wagon train for Galena, Illinois, was not set to leave until

morning. It is 165 miles from Chicago. One can take a stagecoach, the company providing food and overnight stays at posts
along the way, but it costs twelve dollars. A ticket on the wagon
train is half as much. I had already spent thirteen dollars, and
it would be days if not weeks before I reached Shakopee. As I
didn't want to spend money on a room for the night, I asked the
agent if I could sleep in one of the unhitched wagons. He looked
at me as if it was not the first time he'd been asked such a thing,
and to my relief he said that as long as no one else knew about it
and I had no visitors, it was fine with him, although it would cost
me seventy-five cents. I gave him the money, wondering if he
had his own nighttime visit in mind, and what I would do about
that, but he left me alone.

There were three wagons, their canvas roofs unfurled. The
arched frames looked like the rib cages of dinosaurs. Next to the
yard where the wagons were kept were two large pens, one with
eight horses and the other holding two oxen. The smell was very
strong. I made myself a bed in one of the wagons, using my cape
as a pillow.

In the morning, I was awakened by the lurching of the wagon
as it was pulled into the street. A Negro man climbed over the
side, tying what looked like a canvas sail to the frame, all the
while talking to himself. Boys led the horses into the street and
hitched them to the wagon. Large barrels of water were tied to
the sides. I noticed that the wooden wheels, rimmed in iron,
were splintered in places. The men paid me no mind, laughing
and joking as they worked. One boy showed off to a girl in the
street by punching a horse in its face.

By the time the other passengers began to arrive, I had

claimed my seat, nearest to the front. Plank benches along the sides each held six people packed together closely, with their belongings and goods piled in the center. I soon found myself wedged between a husband and wife and their two sickly children, and a salesman who held tightly to a wicker sample case for the entire journey. I offered to help with their youngest child, a two-year-old girl, her face matted with dried snot, but the mother shook her head, holding her out of reach as though I might snatch her away. I kept to myself then, only speaking when necessary, not in need of anyone's companionship or aid. If questioned, I said I was from Philadelphia. Just in case. Ank has tracked me down before.

There were cages of chickens and farm tools and oaken casks, as well as every possession thought necessary for a new life in the West. A waffle iron tied to a child's coffin, and an album of pressed flowers. Perhaps I am unfair. Perhaps that is just what is needed. Some people, I noticed, two men and a woman, carried nothing at all.

Only the children and the sick and aged remained in the wagons when the road led uphill or down, or when the road was too rough, or when the horses were changed, the rest of us walking alongside. There were no springs in the wagons, and each rut and ditch in the road made the children cry and the old people bend double in pain. I had not expected the journey to be pleasurable, but I hadn't imagined that it would be quite so bad.

Most people ran out of food before we reached the Mississippi. I'd bought a bag of cherries, a punnet of apricots, half a loaf of rye bread, and some rotten cheese which was meant to last me five days, but I'd eaten it all by the third day. An elderly

Norwegian woman who was traveling to meet her son in Wisconsin offered to share what was left of her provisions, hard biscuits and a sack of dried apples, but it was not enough for both of us, and I ate only a handful now and then, pretending that I was full. At night, I spread my cape under the wagon, having seen lice on the children and wanting to leave room for the old woman, but it was difficult to sleep with the groans and sobs of my fellow travelers.

We at last reached Galena, bad-tempered and filthy. The old woman was so rattled, so stiff from the journey, I had to ask the help of another passenger, a young man with a cork leg, to lift her from the wagon. I lost her in the crowd, and am ashamed to say I did not try to find her.

At the steamboat office, I bought a ticket to Shakopee, Minnesota, on a riverboat named *The Greek Slave*. The trip upriver will take six days. I spent a half-dollar for two bags of carrots and some cider and a honey cake on the dock, and washed my face and hands in a pump in the street.

. . .

The Galena River is more a wide stream than a river, running east to empty into the Mississippi thirteen miles southwest of the town. The boat is meant for stock rather than passengers, and freight rather than stock. I sleep in a slatted chair in the bow, the hem of my dress stiff with dried mud, which has the advantage of keeping my legs warm at night. My cape covers the rest of me, including my head. Even so, my face and hands are swollen with mosquito bites. There are rats, too, and I keep my feet tucked under me. The cattle, trapped in their sodden pens, moan through the night.

I was told by one of the deckhands, a Negro named Joseph who takes the soundings with lengths of twine, that I am fortunate it was such a mild winter. The ice on the river broke up sooner than is customary. The boats, he said, are drawn off when the water falls low in late summer. I asked him what he did when the boats are not running, and he said he works at the sawmill in St. Anthony when they will have him. There are falls there, twenty feet high and famous around the world. He was surprised I had not heard of them. He said I would do myself a favor by visiting them. He also said he has an Indian wife. When he saw me eating the last of the carrots, he told me that dinner was included in my fare. I pretended that I knew that, but preferred to eat alone. In truth, I was too embarrassed by my appearance, my shabby clothes and dirty hair, and the way that I smelled, to eat with other travelers, even if it was included in my passage.

Near the settlement of Red Wing, three thousand otter pelts were loaded onto the boat by trappers who themselves looked like otters, dressed in skins and fur hats, despite the heat. Old settlements with abandoned houses and trading posts are scattered across the flats, proudly said by Joseph to be a hundred years older than the town of Boston. There are sawmills on the banks, and Indian tipis, arranged in a circle and separated from the settlers' houses by wattle fences. There are quarries of red stone, and thousands of crystals lie scattered at the foot of the bluffs, flashing in the sun. The redbud is in bloom, its leaves a bright scarlet among the river birch and swamp maple. Maddie used to tease me because I knew the names of trees, thanks to the books I read at the asylum.

Men come on board to discuss the state of the river, each with a different view. Some warn about snags, or sandbars, or the danger of the water dropping suddenly. Others find the current a bit strong given the time of year. Stokers disembarking to load wood chased away a grizzly eating the carcass of what might have been a cow and what some said was a man. One night, strong winds caused us to anchor in the middle of the river, the boat shuddering in the stream until the wind shifted and fell away.

I haven't taken in anything new in so long, I don't know where to fix my attention, or even how to see. I have never been more than five miles from the center of Providence. Now I am adrift on a great river, and adrift in my mind. I feel many things at once. Excited and exhausted, calm and distressed. I don't know what to do with so much feeling. My life will now be one of improvisation, forgetting for a moment that my life has always been one of improvisation. I hadn't known how easily a new life may be made. It seems everyone around me is doing the same, gambling that he has chosen the right new life. There are real gamblers on the riverboat, men in striped trousers and doeskin gloves, but you can tell that they, at least, know what they are doing.

.   .   .

We reached Shakopee in Minnesota Territory this afternoon. On the far bank, I could see Indian men on the bluff and women washing clothes in the river.

The Lost Wife

The bandage on my wrist was black with soot, and I unwound it and threw it in the river. The burn is almost healed, but there will be a scar to join my other scars. You must remember this, I said to myself, cleaning the burn with my spit. It is the summer of 1855, and you are free. You are twenty-five years old, and you are a thousand miles from home. What once was home.

Shakopee has a dusty main street with stores and houses on each side, most of them made of unseasoned wood. There are a few brick houses with tin roofs and an Episcopal church with a listing spire, and what appears to be a windowless schoolhouse. There is the smell of cut wood and manure, and the sound of boat horns and the sawing of lumber and the cries of animals as they are prodded from the steamers.

As it was late, I stopped at the first hotel I saw, the Hooper House, where I asked for a room. The clerk sat in a rocking chair with a girl on his lap. He pointed to the stairs, singing, "A bed for a grunt, a bed for a grunt."

I climbed to the second floor, where I found a large open room, crowded with men. The room was full of smoke. There were many beds, most of them occupied. I noticed a rag doll on one of the beds, and a man said, "That's my little sweetheart." There was an empty cot in one corner, separated from the others by a thin cotton sheet nailed to the low ceiling, and I slid my suitcase under it. There was a croker sack stuffed with husks for a pillow and a stained blanket. I was so worn by my journey that I didn't care if the men watched me through the sheet, describing me with great guffaws to those whose view was impeded, disappointed that I did not remove my clothes. They, too, I noticed, slept in their clothes, but I removed my shoes.

. . .

The room was empty when I awoke this morning. A reeking kerosene lantern sat on a table near the door, which did little to dispel the stench from a number of chamber pots overflowing with piss and shit. There is a window high on a water-stained wall, but it is nailed shut.

I changed into the dress I'd kept unworn in my bag and went downstairs. The clerk from last night was playing cards with two men in a dimly lit bar next to the lobby. It was bright outside, no trees or overhanging eaves to deflect the light and the heat, and I regretted that I'd lost my hat. I crossed the street to a small drugstore, reasoning that the pharmacist may have met Maddie, but he had no knowledge of her. He suggested I go to the nearby steamboat office, which kept copies of boat manifests.

I waited in the anteroom of the steamship office for some time before an unruly-looking man asked what it was that I wanted. I said that I was looking for a friend named Maddie Murphy whom I was supposed to meet in Shakopee. He sighed heavily and opened a large ledger, running a tobacco-stained finger down columns of names before turning the page with a wetted thumb. His bent head was close to mine, and the pomade in his hair smelled of fat. He at last stopped and looked at me over the top of his spectacles. He held out his hand and when I realized he wanted money, I gave him a dollar. He said that nine months ago, a Madeline Murphy had died of cholera on board a boat from Davenport called *The Humboldt*. Her body had been carried ashore and buried in a sandbank at the river's edge.

"My dear Maddie," I said. "My dear Maddie."

"Long gone," he said, closing the book with a loud clap. "You won't want the river to drop too low this summer."

. . .

I don't remember leaving the steamboat office or returning to the hotel. Or how I found my way up the stairs and onto my cot.

I could not stop crying. Now and then, someone yelled at me to shut up. During the day, when the men were gone, the room was quiet and no longer thick with smoke. I fell in and out of sleep, unsure if I was dreaming or if I was awake. I had no food. No water. I no longer knew what day it was or how long I had been there. Perhaps three or four days, but I was not sure.

I thought about the asylum and I thought about my mother. Mostly I thought about Maddie.

When I was fifteen, my mother and I were sent to Dexter Asylum for the insane and indigent, where we worked at the asylum's farm for our room and board. We were not separated from those deprived of their reason, most of them Irishwomen dying of heartache, although many of them had surprising and, for the most part, pleasant moments of sanity. We lived there for three years, although the usual time of service is meant to be six months. Some of the men and women had been there for thirty years and would be there until they left in a box.

Before we were sent to Dexter, my mother worked as a chambermaid at a hotel in Federal Hill, best known for its oyster bar, often coming home late and sometimes not at all. She was a saucy woman, small and thin, and I was afraid of her. When she was enraged, which was often, her protuberant blue eyes seemed to swell and her nostrils dilate with each rasping breath. We lived in two rooms in a doss-house in East Providence. I went to the Little Sisters of Mercy for a few hours each day before running home to cook our dinner of cabbage and potatoes. I slept in the kitchen, as the bedroom was for my mother and her guests. It was difficult to sleep because of the noise they made, drinking and carousing in bed, and I preferred it when she did not come home until late. One of her regular customers was a man who had grown rich making tooth powder, and I knew whenever he came to call because he would leave a tin of powder on the stairs for me.

One night, I heard my mother scream, not a playful taunting scream, as I sometimes heard, but a real scream, and I ran into her room. There was a man in the bed. My mother had thrown an oil lamp at him and the bedclothes were on fire. The man jumped from the bed and ran into the street, barefoot and without his trousers, as my mother and I smothered the flames with a blanket. We were already two months behind in rent, and the landlord was relieved to be quit of us. That is when we were sent to Dexter, and I was grateful for it.

I soon made friends with a girl my own age named Maddie. She worked in the vegetable garden and stole whatever she could hide in her bodice, mostly parsley and scallions for us to share at night after lights out. We said that we would give what we did not eat to the other women, but we always ate everything, even the roots.

Maddie was brought to Dexter when she was seven years old

and had grown up there. Her mother and father had died in one of the coffin ships from Sligo, and she'd been found, starving and sick, hiding in a warehouse at India Point, where she was found by the city's dogcatcher. One of the older girls at Dexter taught her to speak English in exchange for an occasional kiss or two, but she taught herself to read and write, sneaking into the usually deserted schoolroom to memorize a primer.

For dinner, we were given white bread and cold tea, even though the storehouses were full of the vegetables we had grown and the cheese and butter we had made, and we were starving. My mother, who was recovering from a bad burn, was given the job of topping carrots and beets, and I was put in the dairy. Once my mother was caught with a sack of parsnips and put in the bridewell for three days. She said she didn't mind her punishment as she did not have to work. My mother was not fond of work.

I made myself indispensable by keeping the dairy's ledgers and receipts. I was proud of my work. I ate butter straight from the churn when no one was looking and licked the cream from the tops of the jugs. One of the feeders liked to pull my hair, but after he told me that cows dream only when they are lying down, I stayed away from him. The men never seemed to bother with Maddie. It was as if her beauty frightened them.

We were given an hour of schooling each morning, taught by two dissolute young men, one of them hairless. Every Thursday, ladies from the town dropped off a box of books as well as old copies of *Burton's Gentleman's Magazine* for the edification of the inmates. Books that were full of words and images unknown to Maddie and me, as well as to everyone else in the asylum, including the schoolteachers. Stories as well as picture books like *Hereditary Scottish Chiefs* and *Bronze Age Crete* and *The Gothic Cathedrals of Lorraine. Lives of the Governors of the State of New York* and, one of my favorites, a three-volume illustrated book of North American trees.

Maddie worried that the ladies would forget to bring the books each week, as she needed to be distracted, needed to be learning something new, which was a way not to be sad. We liked to imagine how some of the books had fallen into the hands of the ladies of College Hill. Perhaps their fathers and husbands were professors or explorers. Some of the books had never been opened, their pages uncut and unseen. That is when I discovered Sir Walter Scott and the Brothers Grimm and Hans Christian Andersen. I also liked reading about famous women of the past, Cleopatra and Mary, Queen of Scots and Anne Boleyn, although not Joan of Arc. I still don't know why Joan was left out, but she was. Maddie said it was because she had no sense of humor, but I don't imagine the women I favored were particularly funny, either. Maddie preferred ghost stories like "The Legend of Sleepy Hollow" and "The Fall of the House of Usher." We were allowed an hour of free time after dinner, and that is when Maddie and I would read. I stole a cheese spreader from the dairy to cut the pages, but it did not do a very neat job. I wished I could steal the books, but we had no place to hide them. When we were through with them, we took them to the schoolroom, where they were put in a closet until the closet became too full and they were thrown into the farm's waste pit. It was

Maddie who taught me that books weren't just for learning, but that you could read because you liked to and to find out things you would never have known otherwise. All my love then went to books. And to Maddie, of course.

Although men and women lived in separate wings of the building and were punished should they meet anyplace other than at work on the farm or in the dairy, my mother found a way to meet men and sometimes women in an empty basement store-room. She was caught when one of the women, whose husband was a favorite of my mother's as he paid in tomatoes, reported her to the matron. We were left at the front gate with three dollars, new shoes two sizes too big, and a warning not to return. It was 1848. My mother was thirty-two years old. I was eighteen.

It took us an hour to walk to Elm Street, where my mother's cousin Peggy worked as cook in the rectory of St. Anne's. She said we could sleep in a shed in the yard, but only for a few nights, as the priest would not like it. I found some old newspapers in the shed, padded my new shoes, and began to look for work. To my surprise, as I had neither looks nor education, and no experience in the world other than counting cows, I found a place within days, working as a sweeper for a jeweler on Dyer Street who allowed me to sleep on a horsehair mattress in the attic of his shop. My mother disappeared.

. . .

I was awakened this afternoon by the hotelkeeper, standing at the end of my bed as he twisted my big toe through a tear in the sheet. He'd come upstairs to see what I was about, a painted

Indian pipe gripped in his teeth, his pale mustache and beard stained pink with tobacco juice. He said I had to quit caterwauling or I'd have to leave. He didn't countenance trouble, especially from females, and I was upsetting his guests. "Besides," he said, "you owe me money." I straightened my dress as best I could and wiped my face with a corner of the blanket. The bed was wet, and I could smell myself as I put on my shoes.

The hotelkeeper followed me down the stairs. He could smell me, too, and he made a face and held his nose. When I asked if there was someplace where I could wash, he pointed to the yard behind the hotel where there was a pump and a bucket. I poured water over my head, wetting myself to the skin and leaving a pool of dirty water at my feet. It was very freshening. My first bath in three weeks.

I paid him the five dollars I owed him and walked to a nearby grocery, where I bought a copy of *The Shakopee Independent*, a bottle of root beer, and a meat pie which was not beef or anything else known to me. The grocer, a thickset man with a stained eye patch, opened the bottle with the heel of his palm, quickly slipping the cap into his overalls pocket as if he feared I would snatch it. I drank the root beer standing at the counter. He seemed not to notice that I was soaking wet.

I finished the pie as I walked from one end of town to the other, waiting for my dress to dry. I had enough money for a few more days of food and five more nights at the hotel. I knew no one. Maddie was dead. There didn't seem to be much of anything between Shakopee and California except rivers and mountains. And Indians. I needed a plan. The thing about running, about impermanence and transience, aside from the simple relief of moving on, is that you don't really have time to think. It is all moving too fast.

My mother understood this. She was good at moving on. I had been working at Mr. Darrow's for four years when one morning she strolled into the shop as if she'd never been away. As if she'd been down the street, gossiping with a neighbor. She said she'd been working as a lady's maid for a recently deceased widow in Pawtucket and was without employment. An Irish porter dragging a large leather case behind him was dismissed with a few coins and a wave of her hand. Her thin manner was meant to emphasize her superiority, and he made a rude gesture behind her back. She was finely dressed in scarlet taffeta, more a ball gown than a day dress. The gown seemed large for her, and I wondered if she had helped herself to the widow's closet when she left. She asked if she could sleep in the attic with me until she found a position suitable to her talents. There were things she could sell in the meantime, shawls and lace and other finery. I said she could stay with me, although I would have to tell Mr. Darrow. Within a few days, she had made herself so useful in a number of ways, some of which I chose to ignore, that Mr. Darrow invited her to stay for as long as she wished. She no longer slept in the attic with me, but in a room alongside the kitchen, where her fancy clothes were hung on pegs. I was most outraged by the bed.

Mr. Darrow had hired an assistant earlier that month, a man in his thirties named Ank Butts who had been apprenticed as a boy to a gem-cutter in New Haven. My work began early, as I had to make a fire in the kitchen and draw water from the well in the yard. One morning, as I bent to light the stove, I heard someone behind me. It was Mr. Darrow's assistant, yawning and rubbing his eyes as my mother pushed him from her room. Not long after, when she tired of him, she sent him upstairs to me.

. . .

There were notices in the Shakopee newspaper for lumbermen and stockmen and skinners and trappers, but nothing for women.

I had to start somewhere. I walked to the drugstore to inquire if they were hiring. The owner gaped at me before announcing that he did not employ women. Had never employed women and would never employ them. "We pride ourselves on our morals here," he said. Sniffing in distaste, he directed me two doors down to a jewelry store where he'd seen a sign in the window offering employment.

I was surprised that there was a jeweler in what seemed to be little more than a trading post. There was another sign in the jeweler's window advertising the treatment of bunions and toothache. I stepped inside. The proprietor, a small, sparsely whiskered man in a dusty black bowler, sat on a stool at the back of the shop, a loupe in one eye. He looked up when I coughed to get his attention, and the loupe fell onto his workbench. I told him I was in need of work and that I'd once worked for a jeweler in Rhode Island. Which was true, although I did not tell him that I can make a ring that is only plated in gold look like real gold and sell it at real gold prices. I told him I had no husband or children and that my mother and father were dead. Which was not altogether true. "Rhode Island is famous for its jewelers," he said, and I wished I'd told him I was from some other place.

At least my lies are reasonable, unlike Maddie's lies. She used to claim that a street in Boston was named after her family. I wonder if I've made up the wrong life.

He asked how I came to be in Shakopee, and I said I'd been making my way to St. Paul to marry my childhood sweetheart when I learned he had forsaken me. To my relief, he wasn't particularly interested. He was interested, however, when I said I was staying at the Hooper House. "They take lady boarders?" he asked in surprise. He said he was a widower and would need to think about hiring me, as he had never worked with a woman, and the ladies of the town were most severe about maintaining decency. He told me to come to his house that evening to discuss it further. He wanted me to know that he lived alone, having taken an early stand against lodgers, as if he feared I aimed to move in with him. I asked him his name. Doc Spankle, he said. When he did not ask me mine, I said that I was called Sarah. He didn't seem to care that I did not have a surname, and I reminded myself that I am in the West now. I don't need a name.

I did as I was bid and walked to his house at dusk, grateful to discover that he had made dinner for us. I apologized for the state of my clothes, explaining that there was no place to wash in private at the Hooper House, and he shrugged and said he was accustomed to a certain lack of hygiene in those passing through town. When I said that I was not passing through town, he gave an odd laugh, more like a bark than a laugh, as if he knew better.

He did not remove his hat as he ground buckwheat to make coffee, straining it through a horsehair sieve. There was cranberry sauce and corn bread with maple syrup, all very satisfying.

I had to remind myself not to eat too fast or I would choke. I wondered if a person could look hungry, and if he saw it in my face. To my relief, he did not behave in such a way as to give offense, although he did ask if he could kiss me when I was leaving. The thought of him without his clothes, but wearing his hat, repelled me. Still, I let him kiss me, the brim of his hat pressed against my forehead.

As I stepped outside, wiping my mouth on my sleeve, three of the town's matrons, one of whom, I later learned, was married to a deacon at the Episcopal church, glared at me suspiciously as I made room for them on the narrow plank sidewalk. It was because of this, I am certain, that I was refused baptism when I began to attend services at St. Anthony's, a sacrament my mother had not troubled to give me and which I thought would be a suitable start to my new life. My attempt at respectability, at least in Shakopee, was useless from the start. Is it any wonder I despise them?

. . .

I dreamed last night that Florence thought Viola was her mother. She did not know that I was her mother. She did not even know my name.

When she was three months old, Ank Butts and I were married at the Orthodox church on Deane Street, so perhaps my mother was right and he was Greek after all. I never asked him. I never asked him anything. We moved to a small corner shop on Eddy Street in the jewelry district. His older sister, Viola, a moody spinster, lived with us above the shop. She was tall, with a small waist and large breasts, and oily dark hair which she wore in snakelike braids coiled around her head. She reminded me of a bee goddess I'd seen in one of the books donated to Dexter. In the beginning, before we had beds, she slept on a mat on the landing, assuming care of Florence the moment she was born, tending her with such felicity that I was able to return to work soon after her birth. I would rush upstairs every few hours to feed her, Viola putting her in my arms with a sigh both envious and fearful, as if I might run off with her and then drop her. Not that she was at fault. She was just following her instincts, as Maddie would say. It was my instincts that were off.

One of Ank's skills, in addition to inflicting pain on women, was in making gold-plated wedding rings, which he claimed were eighteen-karat gold, and jeweled bands set with Mr. Lombardi's glass stones, which he sold as sapphires and rubies. He included engraving in the price of a ring or bracelet, sentimental and sometimes mysterious hieroglyphs like Never Forever, and he taught me to do the engraving. It made me wonder about people, but I was young. That is how I learned the few words of Portuguese and German that I know, words not particularly useful in everyday life like para o túmulo, to the grave, and ein Geschenk von mir, a gift of myself. A gift of myself to the grave. That was my marriage.

My mother left Mr. Darrow's shop soon after my daughter was born, taking with her not only her fine dresses, but his cane with the gold snake and the top hat he wore to funerals. Soon after she left, while cleaning her room, I found in a desk drawer three letters Maddie had written to me in care of Mr. Darrow. I had tried many times to see Maddie at the asylum, standing at the gate in the hope of giving one of the inmates a note for her before I was chased away. I wrote letters to her, but she did not answer them, and I accepted her silence as a sign that she wanted no part of me. When I found her letters in the drawer, I wondered if there had been more letters. She had not abandoned me after all.

The first letter, dated March 1853, was from Lafayette, a small town near Indianapolis. Maddie had run away with one of the schoolmasters at Dexter named Pervis Spykes. They had lived in Lafayette for a year before he lost his job at a boys' school, perhaps, she wrote, because his only experience as a teacher had been a few drunken months at Dexter, instructing inmates who, if they were not insane, could barely speak English, and his method of instruction was a bit lax. They lived together as man and wife, but they were not married. It was possible, although he denied it, that there already was a wife. He had then found a job at a newspaper, thanks to a reference letter he made Maddie write in which she claimed he had worked for the *Providence Weekly Times*. His job for the Lafayette paper was to write death notices and wedding announcements, which was not what he had in mind when applying for the job. He was fired when it was discovered that he made up stories about the dead, describing one prominent woman, the wife of the town's banker, as the love child of P. T. Barnum. He is an unsettled kind of person, she added in a postscript, not able to sustain himself for long at one thing or in one place. When I read the letter, I understood that Maddie, too, was an unsettled person, not because she was restless and unreliable like Mr. Spykes, but because she had no place to settle.

The second letter came from Galesburg, Illinois. It was written six months later. Nothing much had changed, she wrote, except that she was pregnant when they left Lafayette. The baby, a boy, was delivered in a boardinghouse in Peoria by a runaway slave who was a midwife, but died three days after his birth. She wished I had been with her. She wrote that they were headed to Minnesota Territory, where Pervis had heard the government was looking for people to teach in the new schools for Indian children, where the standards were not as strict as those in the schools for white children. She sounded, although I could have been mistaken, as if she was no longer as in need of Mr. Spykes as she once had been.

She had tried to find work at a small library in Lafayette, but she had no experience and, perhaps more important, no education, so could not work in a library where she had most likely read all the books it contained. She had worked in a shoe store and a ball-bearings factory, and as a chambermaid in the boardinghouse where they lived in Peoria in return for their lodging until she grew too apparently pregnant to be useful. It seems to me, she wrote, that whoever lives in the big houses on the shady streets in the towns we pass through—doctors and judges, I imagine—are not on the move, even if the rest of us are in constant motion. Pervis says that is why we are proud to be called Americans. I know what he means. We are an uprooted people, but I don't think we are called Americans because we can't stay in one place long enough to have a nice house on a shady street. The third letter was very brief, written soon after her arrival in Minnesota Territory, in which she told me how to get to Shakopee. And to come soon.

Pervis Spykes's name was not on the boat manifest at the steamboat office. Perhaps he was using an alias. I think Maddie was alone.

. . .

My pay at the jewelry store will be two dollars a week. The first thing I did was to ask Mr. Spankle if he would advance me two weeks' salary so I could move to another hotel, as well as buy a dress and some stockings and a bonnet, also some soap and a toothbrush and tooth powder. He said that he would, although it was against his rules, but suggested that before I do anything, I might avail myself of his outdoor shower. I saw him watching from the back porch as I washed myself, but as I would rather be clean than unobserved, I said nothing. There is a board fence around the shower, so I was able to undress. He could see only my feet and my head and shoulders. It occurs to me that Doc Spankle is looking for a wife.

There were no women's undergarments to be had at Holmes's general store, but I bought a gingham blouse and a skirt, as well as a length of linen and some cheap cotton so that the German tailor on Fuller Street could make me a petticoat and a night-dress. I put aside a half yard of the cotton to cut into monthly pads. I bought for a few pennies one of the reed baskets the Indian women sell by the river and a pair of birch bark slippers. I know the winter will be very cold, but I will think about that later. I left my old tartan cape on a bench in front of the church and then regretted it, but when I went back to get it, it was gone.

There is a Chinese laundry behind the jewelry store, and

I gave them what could be salvaged from my wardrobe to be washed and pressed. I left the Hooper Hotel and moved to a rooming house kept by a woman who sings what she calls very light opera every Saturday night in the saloon in the basement of Mr. Holmes's store. I was given the single room that she keeps for the rare female guest, complete with a washbasin and chamber pot.

Mr. Spankle has a weakness for soliloquy while he works, and I have learned a great deal about him. His ancestors are from the town of Hamelin in Germany. His great-grandfather was the brother of one of the children, a little girl, who disappeared with the Pied Piper when the town refused to pay the piper's fee for ridding Hamelin of rats. Although he tells me other stories, some of which I recognize from a book I read at Dexter called *Memoirs of Extraordinary Popular Delusions,* he has told me the Pied Piper story more than once. It occurs to me that he is trying to make a point. When I asked if he was suggesting I should beware of brightly clothed pipers, he looked up from his work to fix me with two red eyes. "Always pay your debts, my dear. Always pay your debts."

"I have never been so fortunate as to have debts," I said.

"I don't mean money," he said.

I said nothing. Maybe it is true. About the rats.

. . .

I, at least, do not pretend to know anything about dentistry. Or bunions. The screams coming from the back of the store, where Mr. Spankle has bolted to the floor a barber's red leather chair equipped with numerous makeshift straps alongside a deal table neatly laid with what appear to be instruments of medieval torture, including a rusty awl, are often so loud that I know to close the street door whenever the chair is in use.

I first saw Dr. Brinton when he arrived to have a tooth pulled, having previously tried to remove it himself, during which attempt he broke the tooth in half. I knew this because Mr. Spankle requires me to keep an account of all that occurs in the dentistry, lest anyone again expire in his leather chair. I do not know the details of earlier mishaps, as Mr. Spankle tends to be evasive about them, except that a trapper from Lake Traverse died in the chair, supposedly from shock.

Dr. Brinton nodded to me as he left, a bloody handkerchief held to his mouth. I watched from the window as he went down the street to Holmes's store, where I doubted he was stopping to buy boots. I saw him two days later in the drugstore, where I had his attention by knocking over a display of Epsom salts and mineral oil. He helped me across the broken bottles, my shoes spotted with oil, as the furious pharmacist pushed past us with a mop and broom.

Dr. Brinton was a little red in the face, and I wondered if he had been drinking. I noticed that his hands were very clean, not a common sight in Shakopee. He is fastidious in his dress as well, and when he lifted a trouser leg so it would not be soiled, I saw that his sock was blue with white polka dots. I could see an undershirt beneath his linen shirt. He is, of course, a gentleman. A bit conceited, perhaps. A very tall, clean-shaven, almost handsome gentleman, with sly gray eyes set a little too far apart in a face the color of wet sand. He wondered if he had perhaps come across me in town, as I seemed familiar, and I said if that were so, I would surely have remembered meeting him. There was no reason to lie. It seems my mother was right. I cannot help myself.

I apologized to the pharmacist, offering to pay for the broken bottles, which I did not for a moment intend to do, but Dr. Brinton interrupted me to give the man a quick look, which I took to mean he would pay my debt. As he walked me to the corner, past the jewelry store, where I was late for my afternoon shift, he stopped suddenly and said, "I must turn back, I've forgotten some medicine, distracted by your performance." When I gave him my hand in goodbye, I saw him look at the scars on my wrists and forearms.

I thought, This will be easy.

. . .

I knew that Mr. Spankle had been married in Shakopee and I asked him what papers had been required. He said no papers had been needed, although he'd been asked to swear on the Bible that he was Doc Spankle. Well, he said after a moment, Theophilus Spankle.

I can do that, I thought. Swear that I am Sarah Brown. Or perhaps Becky Sharp, after one of my favorite characters. Or Jane Eyre. No one would know otherwise, except perhaps the doctor. I decided that I would be Sarah Brown. Or rather Browne. The "e" giving it distinction.

When I asked Mr. Spankle if he'd had to remove his hat, he threw a polishing rag at me.

Dr. Brinton was late for our wedding, having spent the morning at the Masonic lodge with his friend, the Indian agent Major Weems, drinking beer and eating oysters. Arguing, he said, about the Kansas-Nebraska Act of last year, which would allow the western territories to become slave states. He did not say which side he favored. I wondered if he was drunk because he was afraid he might change his mind about becoming my husband and catch the next steamboat to St. Paul.

He'd been drinking the afternoon I suggested we marry, too. He did not answer my proposal, but asked me to his rented house on Union Street. He took me into his bedroom. There was no chair and I sat on the bed. As he unbuttoned his fly, letting his trousers fall to his ankles, he said that he should perhaps warn me that he had only one testicle, but that it did not impede ejaculation or, for that matter, pleasure. I said that I was happy his condition did not impede satisfaction, although he'd said nothing about my own, which made him laugh. He poured a solution of what he said was cardamom, brandy, and pulverized green beetle, more commonly known as Spanish fly, from a jug he kept under his bed into a bowl, and then lowered his one ball into it.

We both watched to see what would happen. After a few undecided moments, his cock began to get hard, and he dropped the bowl, pulled up my skirt, and fell on top of me. It was not unlike the game that Maddie and I used to play at the asylum, complete with dirty words.

That I was not a virgin did not seem to trouble him, if he

even noticed. What mattered was that I hadn't been shocked or repelled and that his cock was hard. I wasn't repulsed, it's true, but I wasn't aroused, either, but that mattered only to me, and not very much. It was an improvement over my first time with Ank Butts, my mother shouting from the bottom of the stairs to stop bawling and get on with it.

.   .   .

He gave me money for a wedding dress, and the tailor made me a hooped gown of cream-colored piqué with pagoda sleeves and a lace dickie, a little tight yet maidenly. There was money to spare, and I bought a pair of gray boots with elk-horn buttons. Mr. Spankle loaned me his dead wife's Canton shawl, which I pinned to the back of my head. He reminded me several times to return it by morning, as if her ghost might object to his generosity. He walked me to the registry, his eye on the shawl, causing the gossips of the town to think that he was the groom.

My new husband did not wish to celebrate, and we retired to his little house, where he fell onto the bed, his hands behind his head. "I want to watch you undress," he said. "We haven't done that."

He fell asleep as I removed my boots. I felt in his jacket pockets for a ring, Mr. Spankle having offered him a discount, but there was no ring, only a small brown glass bottle, a pair of gold-framed eyeglasses, and some money, which I kept. I went barefoot into the kitchen, my dress billowing around me, and ate some cherries I found in a bowl in the sink. I was suddenly ravenous, leaning over the sink so as not to stain my dress as I stuffed my mouth with cherries, spitting the pits into the drain until the sink was red with juice.

. . .

My husband is a graduate of Yale College Medical Institution, the son of a distinguished doctor from a New England family. His brother is a lawyer in nearby Blue Earth. Despite his seemingly frank manner, there is something inaccessible about him. His surprising fits of temper are in contrast to that side of his nature which is calm and gentle. It sometimes seems as if he is two men, each appearing at shorter and shorter intervals, moments of violence alternating with states of euphoria. When I have something to tell him, he always asks, "Is that so?" neither believing nor disbelieving me. He did ask how I came to be in Minnesota Territory of all places in the country, and I told him I'd been engaged as a schoolteacher in the town of Jordan, but arrived only to discover that the schoolhouse had burned down. I said that all of my family had died in the Rhode Island cholera epidemic of 1854. He seemed relieved by this sad news, as if he had no desire for more relatives, or perhaps it was only none of mine. I wished I had not said Rhode Island, but it was too late. He said nothing, only removed his spectacles to stare at me.

My new husband is generous. With the money remaining after I bought my wedding dress and boots, I bought two pairs of cotton stockings and a length of rose-colored wool and some green plaid silk, as well as four yards of lavender linen and a pair of green suede gloves. Also some Queen of Hungary water and a cotton shawl. The tailor made me a winter dress and a skirt from the silk, and two bodices, one in the plaid and the other in linen. I have never had a silk skirt before. Or silk anything, for that matter. I wear the plaid when Dr. Brinton and I walk to the jetty to await the arrival of the day's last steamboat. There are not many places to go in town, although we sometimes make our way to Mr. Holmes's sawmill, as the wood smell is very pleasant in the warm evening air. His step is often faltering, and I've noticed that he takes frequent sips from the brown glass bottle he carries in his pocket. When he saw me watching him, he frowned and said he is much given to migraine. I have never seen my husband drunk, but he is never quite sober.

I once overheard him tell Major Weems that he left his medical practice in New Haven to work in the California gold fields, where he remained for five years, caring for the miners and whores and Chinamen until he, too, fell ill with cholera. There were other ailments, one with which I am familiar. The clap has left his cock marked with red scars, caused by the application of silver nitrate, which he did not mention to Major Weems. Or that he has only one testicle. I tell him that it makes no difference to me, but men never believe you about such things.

I do not know what brought him to Shakopee, other than the presence of his brother. Or rather, what has kept him here. He was very sick when he arrived from San Francisco, I know. Perhaps he was on his way home to Connecticut, but could go no farther in his condition. Or perhaps he chose to end his journey, undeterred by the town's mixture of coarseness and prudery. I sometimes wonder if he, too, is running from something.

He is the only physician in Shakopee. He uses a barn as a clinic, despite its dirt floor and the lingering smell of hay and dust. He sees the people of the town, mostly men, and sometimes Indians, who appear only when they have been wounded in an attack or otherwise injured. Now and then a lady picks her way gingerly across the gravel yard and looks over her shoulder before she disappears inside. He is intent on vaccinating Shakopee's children for smallpox, which has not been easy, given the resistance of many parents.

I am a plain woman. I admit that. I have no particular charms or gifts, no distinguished ancestors, no education except what I gleaned from books about the Spanish armada or Gothic churches. My life has left me both innocent and crude. Humiliation has not improved my nature. The idea that suffering teaches kindness is not necessarily true.

No one knows anything about me, including my husband. Sometimes I am tempted to tell him the truth, although what version of the truth I do not know, so I say nothing. The question is not why I chose him. I know the answer to that. The question is why he allowed me to choose him. That will always be a mystery. Soon after our marriage, when it was still permissible, if not pleasantly provocative to wonder aloud, I asked him why he had married me. He pretended to misunderstand and said, "It is always a mistake to assume that men want their freedom. That is why habit is so alluring."

One afternoon when he hurried from the house to attend a woman in labor, he left his jacket behind. I found the glass bottle in a pocket and took a sip. It was both sweet and harsh, tasting of nutmeg. I rinsed my mouth, but the taste remained, and the smell of it, and I rinsed my mouth again.

He is drinking laudanum.

The Lost Wife

. . .

Three times a week, when the mail arrives with the stagecoach, Dr. Brinton collects the newspapers and journals and letters addressed to him, some from as far distant as London and Heidelberg. He corresponds with several old friends, many of them from medical school, and every month there is a fat letter from his mother, recounting in detail the gossip of Winsted, Connecticut. I know because I read the letters when he is asleep. There is never any mail for me, which of course he has noticed, but he says nothing. I am going to subscribe to some ladies' magazines, if only to have some mail.

There was a young Indian girl at the dock this evening, weeping quietly and wringing her hands. The passengers had disembarked and the freight and stock been unloaded, but she would not leave, even when the women called her from the riverbank. The ship's captain leaned from the gangplank and spoke to her in Dakota. I did not understand what they said to each other, but he disappeared into the main cabin and returned a few minutes later carrying a small black dog, which he gave to her. It seems the cook had stolen it from her earlier in the week.

May 1862

I HAVE TRAVELED SO FAR and to places so unfamiliar that I have a hard time keeping my geography straight. It helps me to think of the rivers. The Redwood, the Cottonwood, the Mississippi, the Minnesota, the Yellow Medicine. Each day, I remind myself where I am, lest my story grow confused. It is the second year of the War in the South. I am Mrs. Sarah Brinton. I am thirty-two years old. I have been married for seven years to Dr. John L. Brinton. He is forty years old. We live at the Indian agency in Yellow Medicine, where my husband is the resident doctor, tending the Sioux on the nearby reservation, as well as the men who work at the agency and their families. I have two small children, James, who is four years old, and my Anne, who will soon be two. She is learning to talk. I dote on my children, too much so, according to my husband, but I cannot help myself. I have much to amend. I am terrified that they will fall from the bluff, or be killed by a rattlesnake, or attacked by one of the timber wolves that roam about the agency. They are always with me, as if that will save them.

We arrived here last June, traveling west by steamboat from Shakopee to Mankato, where we joined a wagon train, our belongings following on three oxcarts. The distance from Mankato to the Upper Agency is more than a hundred miles, following the river past the Indian villages of Mankato, Little Crow, Chief Shakopee, and Big Eagle. At Redwood, I looked at the one log hut and the seven hundred Indians camped at the river's edge, and thought, Is this where I am to live? I cannot live in such a place. I was relieved to learn that it was only a stopping post.

We made ourselves as comfortable as possible in a covered wagon drawn by two horses, which was not easy, the restless children huddled under a mosquito net in the back of the wagon. At night, Dr. Brinton slept on the ground, as he is too tall to sleep in a wagon. I was unable to sleep, certain the Indians were only waiting until dark to cross the river to kill us.

In the morning, the teamsters brought us water, and we washed ourselves as best we could and made tea and ate apples and hard biscuits before continuing our journey. Every few miles, we climbed from the wagon so that the horses could be coaxed through a slough. Then we would climb back onto the wagon until we reached the next ditch. The first sign of real habitation—that is, white habitation—was a small brick house near the Redwood River, which I was told was a schoolhouse for Indian children, two rooms below and a room above where the schoolteacher, a man of mixed descent named Renville, lives with his wife and children. I could hear the voices of the pupils as they read from their primers in halting English, but I saw no one.

We followed the winding dirt track, lurching in and out of the deep ruts and struggling up and down a series of high bluffs. We reached the Yellow Medicine River at dusk on the third day and entered a fertile valley with rounded hills said to be Indian mounds and a large village of perhaps two hundred tipis. I could see women bathing in the river and men sitting on the ground in groups, smoking pipes. There was the sound of drums. Dr. Brinton said it was a Wahpeton camp. I had not expected such beauty, and for an instant, I thought, Oh, I could be happy here.

Major Weems, the Indian agent, was waiting for us. The agency looked like a fort, as he had decorated it with banners, and torches had been lit to mark our arrival. With Lincoln's election, new agents had been appointed, among them Major Weems, who insisted that my husband be given the post of doctor at the agency, where he would be paid a thousand dollars a year. It is preferable, Dr. Brinton said, to working in the gold fields. When I asked what he'd been paid in California, he looked surprised. "A nugget or two," he said with a smile. "They didn't have much."

Our first night, I could hear the Indians playing their drums and singing, and I feared it was our death song. It grew silent near dawn, and I was at last able to sleep, only to be awakened by a loud stamping and pounding on the porch. Dr. Brinton went into the yard with his pistol, where he discovered that the agency's horses, which had been let out for the night, had come into the yard in the hope of escaping the mosquitoes. There was not an Indian in sight.

. . .

Our house is on a bluff, five hundred feet above the valley, overlooking the meeting of the Yellow Medicine and Minnesota Rivers. There is a brick warehouse, half of which serves as my husband's dispensary and the other half as the agency's office. Major Weems lives in a house nearby with his wife, Henrietta, and their young children, Jacob and Estelle. There are four trading stores for the use of the Indians, two of them owned by a former butcher named Hilly Gamp. Nearby are barracks for the agency workers, some of them men of mixed descent, and a jail in which there are always two or three noisy inmates. Dr. Brinton says there are fewer agency workers than usual as the men have gone to the War. This week, one of the blacksmiths and two stockmen left to join the Union Army. Another man disappeared after announcing his intention to fight with the rebels, leaving behind his Sisseton wife.

There is yet another school for Indian children. The teacher is a man of Canadian and Sisseton blood who does not teach them to read and write, but instructs them in manual skills such as carpentry and farming. There is a privy behind our house, a large enclosed yard with a well, stone troughs for washing, and an ice cellar. Our nearest white neighbors, a Swedish farmer named Axel Berggren and his family of five sons, live in a log house a mile away. There is a tipi in their yard where the farmer and his oldest son hold frequent councils with the Sisseton chiefs.

The braves are tall and handsome with strong, beaked noses, their black eyes set wide in their long faces. They are lanky and erect, proud of bearing, quick to take offense and quick to laugh. They pride themselves in maintaining a blank expression, their wishes conveyed by a forceful gesture rather than speech, which frightened me at first. I sense that despite their reserve, they are emotional, even volatile. I often hear them laughing, I suspect about us.

They are without beards or any hair that I can see except eyebrows and what is on their heads, where it is sometimes bound with red cloth and sometimes twisted into a topknot tied with feathers and coins. Sometimes they rub soot in their hair to darken it. Any hair on the face or the body is removed using hinged mussel shells from the river. Some of them wear striped turbans made from cloth sold by the traders which they pierce with feathers. Others wear roaches of horsehair or porcupine quills dyed red with buffalo berries, attached to their heads with leather straps. To my surprise, the white tubular ornaments known as hair pipes and which they string in necklaces come from, of all places, New Jersey.

A blanket is fastened at the left shoulder and tucked under the right arm to leave one arm free. Their deerskin leggings reach to the thigh, attached to a waistband by thin straps or held by garters tied at the knee. Flaps at the bottom of their leggings are tucked under each foot. They sometimes wear only a breech-cloth, a long strip of tanned deerskin looped between their legs and fastened at the waist. In the back, there is little more than a string between their buttocks, and when a man bends over, he might as well be naked. I notice that the white women, including myself, try not to stare, afraid of what they might see. Sometimes I must force myself to look away.

The women are winsome, especially when young and before they have been worn by work, never raising their eyes, their heads lowered. Their legs are unusually long, which makes them appear short-waisted. They hold the edge of their robes to their mouths when they speak, which makes it difficult to hear them. Many of the old women are bent nearly in two, having for years carried heavy burdens with straps placed across their foreheads. Both the men and women have black tattoos of animals and stick figures and mysterious geometric designs. Some have two blue lines tattooed down their chins so that when they die the Owl Maker will not chase them from the Ghost Road. On the older men and women, the tattoos are faded, as if the dye has seeped deep into their skin.

At first, the children would hide in the hazel bushes when they saw me in the yard, but now they pull on my skirt to ask for crackers and bacon. James is busy with them all day, running in and out of the house. They do not wear clothes until they are nine or ten, and James wonders why he must wear a shirt and pants. Sometimes at night, the children hide in his bed, and I must find their mothers to take them home.

The women were the first to come to the house, cautious and silent, and I engaged three of them. There are now eight Dakota women with me throughout the day. They have taught me to make pemmican, which I find most delicious, although I am convinced no white person can prepare it properly, and they have shown me the way to coax a smoky lavender dye from the blue paper cones used to wrap sugar. They bring me branches of juniper to burn when the wind is from the north and the stink of Mr. Gamp's piggery is strong, and baskets of wild plums more succulent than peaches, and I give them flour and beef and eggs. There is cooking to be done, and canning, and the butchering and smoking of fish and pork and game, and laundry to be washed and pressed (my husband is particular about his clothes). The women sew and cook for me, which is considered corrupting; not that they are given work, but because I pay them. I must admit, I like getting into a made bed. My life is one of ease—I am warm in the winter, never hungry, with the luxury of a bathtub and a clean privy. I have servants. I'm gentry now. Who would have thought it.

Our house is dark inside, not only because of the mahogany furniture his mother has sent us but because the Sisseton like to stand at the windows, sometimes two or three deep, to watch us, chatting about us in Dakota and laughing at us, sometimes uproariously. When they are not at the windows, they come inside without knocking or invitation to ask for food or simply to keep us company. They like to twine James's pale hair between their fingers, amused by his curls and by his fearlessness, which they esteem even more than his hair.

I sometimes cannot distinguish one man from another, although I am beginning to know the women very well. Of course, there are good Indians and bad Indians. All their wicked habits—drinking and cursing and stealing—have been learned from the traders, who steal from them, and take their women, then desert them when they tire of them. The traders give them the rusty rifles purchased from the English thirty years ago in exchange for their finely painted and quilled robes.

As the Sioux know no recourse for their wrongs but war, their humiliation makes for the sense of danger I cannot help but feel, present just beneath the surface, waiting to erupt. It is also possible that I exaggerate and have nothing to fear. Still, I am ill at ease around the men. I am convinced that the locks of hair decorating their shirts and leggings are the hair of people they have killed. The amused women tell me that the hair is their own, woven for the most honored of the braves by their mothers and sisters, but I do not believe them. Dr. Brinton, who knows about such things, says they believe that hair is part of the soul because it continues to grow after death. If the scalp of a fellow warrior is taken, he cannot enter the Land of the Great Spirit until an enemy scalp is taken in return. I tell him I don't care to know any of this.

. . .

Our house has a front parlor and a dining room, both rooms crowded with furniture. The parlor has olive-green walls, said to be a fashionable color, and three windows which open onto the yard. There is a kitchen with a black stove and an enamel sink. There are two bedrooms upstairs and a closet with a tin bathtub. Dr. Brinton and I sleep in a four-poster bed which is too short for him, causing him to grumble in his sleep.

I have never had furniture of my own. I've never had a carpet, and although the house is a bit cramped with all the things his mother has sent, it makes me feel proud. There are two Japanese vases in the parlor, painted with cranes, in which I keep stalks of the bluestem grass that grows on the prairie, although I'm sure Mrs. Brinton would prefer peacock feathers. Not one, but two Chinese carpets. Two lithographs, one by an artist named José Baturone, *Típos Californianos: An Excellent Segar,* and the other of Lola Montez, with the inscription "A mi amigo, Juan, San Francisco 1852," which belong to my husband. There is a piano shawl, although no piano yet. There are three stuffed Baltimore orioles under a glass bell. Sometimes I wonder what to make of it all. What is it good for? What am I to do with it? Then I collect myself and invite Mrs. Weems to tea.

It takes me days to compose thank-you notes sufficiently formal to match Mrs. Brinton's gifts as well as her expectations. It is another instance of the benefits of reading, as it was Jane Austen who taught me how to write a thank-you letter. My mother-in-law wonders when she will meet her grandchildren. I am very careful in these matters. She would want to know too much. There have already been questions as to who my people might be. My husband told me that she feels particularly honored that her mother's grandfather was with the English at Fort William Henry when Montcalm and his Iroquois allies massacred hundreds of the fort's defenders and their wives and children after they surrendered.

Dr. Brinton is writing what is called a monograph on the Santee, or Eastern Dakota. They are comprised of four groups, the Mdewakanton, who lived near us in Shakopee and are most familiar to me, the Wahpeton, the Wahpekute, and the Sisseton, with whom we live now. He says that long ago they were rice gatherers in the north until the Ojibwe drove them onto the prairie with guns given them by the French. They move camp according to the season, and in pursuit of game. He admires their fearlessness, their resourcefulness, their fortitude. Their way with horses. "Their good looks," he said with a smile. "Not a trait necessarily required for killing buffalo."

"I am afraid of them for the same reasons," I said.

He asked if I had ever seen an Indian before coming west. "Surely there are Indians in Rhode Island. The Pequot and the Narragansett."

I said of course there are Indians in Rhode Island, but I didn't know any.

"My great-grandfather kept two Pequot children as slaves, although my father denied it. They were servants, he said, not slaves." It was one of the few times he'd ever spoken about his father, who died with his favorite dog and a woman not his wife in a mysterious boating accident in Maine.

"How do you know they were slaves?" I asked, a bit shocked.

"My great-grandfather left them to his daughter in his will. 'Jack, the Indian boy, age nine.'"

It is true, I knew very little about Indians when I arrived in Shakopee seven years ago. I still know very little. I had read about Indians, of course, in James Fenimore Cooper, as well as Mary Rowlandson's account of her abduction, and that of Mary Jemison, and I had heard the story of Eunice Williams who was captured in Deerfield and chose to stay with her captors, but nothing prepared me for my life now, the Santee my constant companions. I allow the chiefs to sit at my mother-in-law's dining table—more than that, I invite them inside to eat with us. Corn fritters and cherry cobbler and pork patties. Smoked trout and black currant cordial. Dr. Brinton is amused that several of them now insist on having their own linen napkins. They eat when they are hungry, but as they have observed our curious habit of eating at regular times, they arrive just as we are sitting down. They eat so hungrily that they soon grow sleepy and forget any mischief they may have had in mind. One of our guests wears two long rattlesnake skins, one tied to each wrist, which he removes before dining, leaving them on the sofa until he has had his fill. He then asks me to retie them to his wrists, which I do. I don't intend my admiration of them to be a mark of condescension. Their splendor is only the most visible part of them. The idea of who is civilized and who is not seems to refer to many things, religious customs, and what stories we tell, and the way food is prepared, and how the defeated in battle are treated. Even table manners.

Sometimes I give them food to take to their tipis, as I know from the women that they are running short of provisions. Now and then I find they have taken something from the larder. I can tell when they help themselves to sugar, as it crunches underfoot where it has spilled.

I already know many words in Santee, having lived in Shakopee for six years, but my vocabulary is becoming more refined, more precise. The women present the words to me like gifts, which is what they are. Although they are familiar with grouse and prairie chickens, they had never seen a rooster, which they find admirable in its noisy defiance, calling it an-pay-ho-to-no, or voice of the morning. My mirror is named minne-odessa, or it looks like water. I am a tall woman with ample girth, made heavier by childbearing, my breasts still full with milk. Their name for me is Tanka-Winohinca-Waste, which means large good woman. I am certainly large. I am still nursing, although my husband encourages me to wean our daughter. He says that she will be slow to walk, as I insist on carrying her throughout the day and lie next to her at night until she falls asleep. Still, he trusts my judgment, always a bit of a surprise, given my past, but he doesn't know about that. It is not because he has faith in me, but because he reserves his judgment for matters he considers more important.

I have made a vegetable garden behind the house with their help. I have never had a garden before. Although some of the Indians, those called Friendlies by the whites, have been taught by the missionaries to plant corn and potatoes and other vegetables, the Dakota on the reservation cultivate nothing, not even tobacco, as they are what Dr. Brinton calls nomadic. The women had never sowed seeds before. Now we grow beets and carrots and a purple bean which is a bush and does not need staking. Also West Indian gherkins for pickling and crookneck squash. I planted a border along either side of the path that leads from the bluff with the cuttings of a prairie rose I found at the edge of the woods, as well as baptisia, wild indigo, and the native prairie smoke with its whorls of pink flowers. Also a wildflower, which the women call rattlesnake master. Dr. Brinton asked me to plant wild bergamot, which the Santee use to treat vomiting, and purple coneflower, which relieves pain. He shares it with the veterinarian, who gives it to horses.

This bounty is thanks to Dr. Brinton, I do admit that. And thank him for it. There is his government pay, of course, but he has money of his own, which he allows me to spend as I like. He is honorable about money, paying his debts, mostly to booksellers, and my own debts, even when I have gone a bit mad, ordering lace fichus and glass lampshades. A woman's bicycle. Chocolate Easter eggs.

I now have three pairs of shoes. Maddie would be jealous.

And then steal them. Sometimes when I order things from the East, a dressing gown or a silver reticule, I try to imagine what Maddie would like and then I buy it for her. A man's tweed cap and a black cape, for example. When I first knew Maddie, she wore her blond hair in a braid down her back, never undoing it as it was too difficult to wash with the scant amount of soap we were allowed. When she was caught stealing radishes, a matron cut off her braid so close to her scalp that she was often mistaken for a boy, a confusion that she exploited to her advantage, once serving as an altar boy so as to drink the wine.

Some days I am quite fond of my husband. The Dakota name for him is Patan. "To save." The Dakota have not forgotten that a few years ago in Shakopee, he saved the lives of many of them wounded in an attack by the Ojibwe, his own hair matted with blood and tissue as he labored through the night. He has learned many things from them and seeks to learn more. He prescribes white cedar bark for stomach ailments and oak bark tea for diarrhea, even dispensing them to his white patients. Calamus root for toothache. Male sage for coughs and colds and for regulating blood sugar. (I don't know about female sage.) He has submitted a paper on native medicine to his former medical school in New Haven.

There is a copper still behind the house, built by a brazier from Tennessee, but he left in May to join the rebels in Chattanooga, and the still is silent. A whumping sound was made as the corn turned to mash, and James thought that demons were trapped inside the still. Dr. Brinton keeps the last three kegs behind the stairs in his dispensary to drink with Major Weems when they play checkers. Sometimes I spy on them. That is when I learn things—things I wish I didn't know. Two years ago, before his wife traveled from Pennsylvania to join him, Major Weems kept a young Sisseton girl in his rooms. There was a child who died, and Dr. Brinton saw that the girl was returned to her people. Last night, Major Weems asked my husband if he knew where he might find the girl, and my husband said he had not seen her since she left Shakopee. I could tell from his voice that he was lying.

.   .   .

There are a number of surveyors staying at the agency. They leave ax marks on certain trees in the valley to designate the boundaries and quadrants of their maps. The Dakota feel the deepest hatred for them, knowing that their presence means more intrusion on their land. They dash their ponies at them, stopping just short of harming them, although it is considered a coup if they can knock over their tripods.

We brought thirty-nine hens with us from Shakopee. They are kept in the barn as soon as there is a hard frost, but in the spring and summer they roost in the hazel hedge. Anne has a fondness for them and speaks to them in a language they seem to understand. A golden cockerel and an irritable rooster fight over her, following her onto the porch and tapping with their beaks on the front door when she goes inside. The men at the agency like to race the hens, betting on them and scaring them into a frenzy. It is hard to make a chicken walk a straight line, which is perhaps the point. So far, the longest length of time a hen has been recorded in flight is eight seconds, earning twenty cents for her backer, Mr. Flanagan. It is James's job to catch the chickens when they stagger past the finish line.

We occasionally lost a hen when we were first here. I thought that foxes were carrying them off, but no longer. Last week, I saw a hen in the basket of a Sisseton woman, but I said nothing. Major Weems told my husband that Flipper Jaxson the skinner has fallen in love with one of the black-and-white hens and keeps her in his hammock, but my husband pretended not to understand him. That is another thing I like about him. It's not that he is offended by bestiality, just not very interested.

.   .   .   .

No one here, I've noticed, wears underclothes. When I gave one of the teamsters Dr. Brinton's old tweed coat, he said it was the first coat he'd ever owned. In the winter, when it can reach eighteen below, they wear padded trousers and four or five shirts, but few of them possess coats. I don't know how they bear the cold. I wear a pair of my husband's wool trousers under my skirt, two flannel shawls, a fur hood, and several sweaters, but that is inside. I try not to leave the house in winter.

As well as the dining table and chairs and carpets and bedsteads sent by my mother-in-law, some of it in pieces when the oxcarts at last reach us, this last winter she thoughtfully included a packing case of bran in which were two bonnets, one for winter, one for summer, a silk parasol lime green in color, and a dozen pairs of white lace mittens much prized, she would be surprised to learn, by the Sisseton women. Several illustrated ladies' magazines were tucked around the hats, perhaps to assure me they were in the latest style, as well as quite a few pamphlets of Christian homilies, as if she fears I am neither fashionable nor godly, both of which assumptions would be true. Last fall, she sent five dozen tulip bulbs, which I planted, but they have yet to bloom.

I am grateful for all that she has sent, even if I have little use for the hats or the parasol or the mittens. I wore one of the hats to a dance in Fort Ridgely—a Prussian blue silk with pale gray grebe feathers, and a delicate frill of Alençon tucked beneath the brim. The bearded fiddlers who played through the night danced while they fiddled, leaping about like goats. The dancing made the feathers in my bonnet tremble. Dr. Brinton does not dance, but I hoped he was watching me, only to discover he was drinking with the fort's chaplain.

I am going to give pretty Henrietta Weems one of the bonnets, the one with the gray grebe feathers. It will suit her blue eyes. She told me she was born in a small Pennsylvania town near the Susquehanna River, one of seventeen children. Her father was a farm laborer. When he was killed in a hunting accident, her mother moved to Harrisburg and opened a boardinghouse. Major Weems was one of her lodgers. She said she had eight older sisters, some of whom needed husbands before she could be wed, but Major Weems insisted that she be his wife and she was happy to oblige him. He promised her a wedding chest when they married, although she has yet to see it. She said there were many secrets in her family. Dreadful sins, committed by her brothers upon her sisters. She has a certain innocence that I envy—she really thinks that owls are wise and snakes are mean, and I do not disabuse her. I find that I am sometimes irritated by this, as if it is dangerous to me.

Her house is certainly not what I would call clean, but she does not seem to mind, perhaps the result of having sixteen brothers and sisters. I suggested that she ask one of the Dakota women to help her, at least with the children, but she is not interested. She knows only one word in their language, ogu, which means maybe. As opposed to Mrs. Flanagan, the blacksmith's wife, who knows only hunta yo, get out of the way. When I asked if she was afraid of the Dakota women, she said, somewhat mysteriously, "Oh no, they have such lovely voices."

If it were not for Henrietta, I would not have realized how much I have missed the companionship of another human creature. That is, a white person. Although I am rarely alone, and although I have grown fond of many of them, friendship with a Santee woman is not quite the same thing. I learn things from Henrietta, not that she sees fit to teach me, but because I watch what she does. For example, she is polite to Mrs. Flanagan, not because she deserves her respect, but because it is less wearing to be courteous than to be vexed. Mrs. Flanagan claims that she read in a newspaper that Indians use dogs' tongues as dishcloths, which surprised me as I did not know she could read.

One morning when I was teaching two women to iron, Henrietta noticed the scars on my wrists. I said that I had been burned in a factory accident, and she leaned over and kissed one of the scars. "My sister Georgie did that, too," she said. "Only she did it in the privy, and when Ephraim found her, he pissed on her." At my look of shock, she put her hands to her face and began to cry.

.   .   .

The newspapers from St. Anthony arrived this afternoon, brought by one of the drovers.

Dr. Brinton read an article from *The Weekly Pioneer and Democrat* aloud to me. "On the fourteenth of May, the pilot of a Confederate steamer anchored in Charleston Harbor, a twenty-three-year-old slave named Robert Smalls, seized the ship with his fellow slaves while the ship's officers were onshore, taking on board his wife and children and several other families, and sailed with them to the Union navy." He asked Major Weems into the dispensary to celebrate the news, but Major Weems made his excuses, not liking to extoll someone of color, he said, so my husband invited me to drink a toast with him instead.

As I sat with him in the dispensary, it occurred to me that perhaps he lied to Major Weems about the Indian girl because he himself sees her. As I watched him cross and recross his legs, I felt myself grow warm with jealousy, and was embarrassed for myself.

.   .   .

Last night, we were startled by the sudden sound of clashing spears and hatchets. Dr. Brinton shoved the children under a table, both of them screaming, more at being pushed under a table than by the clamor outside, and I crawled to a window. There was a full moon and I could see clearly into the yard.

There at the grindstone were forty men in feathers and war paint, waiting patiently to sharpen their weapons. Some of the men were mounted, while others squatted around the stone. Sparks flew from the blades, illuminating for an instant their painted faces. My only fear was that Major Weems would make trouble by chasing them away, but his house was dark and he did not appear.

Plumed centaurs in the moonlight. I had not been aware that I have a romantic nature.

.   .   .

John Roland, a quarrelsome defrocked French Canadian priest who works for the agency as bookkeeper, complained to my husband that a white woman was not born to sit on the ground smoking a pipe with Indians. Dr. Brinton repeated this to me without censure, although he did not hesitate to hit me earlier this week for dancing too feverishly with a half-Indian trapper at a dance in the warehouse. A Sisseton woman, alarmed at hearing James scream, tried to enter the house, but Mrs. Flanagan chased her from the porch and could hardly wait to tell her friends that Dr. Brinton had beaten his wife. It was reported in the St. Anthony newspaper as the unfortunate result of too much merriment at a cornhusking party. The headline read "Why Should the Government Pay Him to Beat His Wife?" The paper demanded that my husband be fired, but for once Major Weems and I were in agreement, and we denied that he had beaten me.

No unseemly quarrels, no innocent misunderstandings, only sudden eruptions of inexplicable fury. I keep a small pair of scissors in my pocket, something I have not done since my mother and I were thrown out of the asylum.

.   .   .

Four miles from the town of Shakopee, not far from Eden Prairie, there is a large boulder called Red Rock, which the Dakota consider sacred. It is said to have come from the Pipestone Quarry, where the Indians believe the rocks were stained red by the blood of the thousands of Indians said to have drowned there. Although it is now on settlers' land, they visit the site to fast and to dance and to leave offerings, especially when they are at war with the Ojibwe. As soon as they leave, the whites steal anything of value left behind, which explains Major Weems's glass cabinet of artifacts.

There was a larger stone near Lake Minnetonka, but it was taken at night by a doctor from St. Louis and given to a museum. The Mdewakanton chief Little Crow asked my husband if he could find the stone and return it to them. Of course he could not, and he truthfully told him that a doctor had stolen it. Chief Little Crow and his braves were enraged, shouting their war cries as they wheeled their trembling ponies in the yard, but there was nothing to be done.

Little Crow is a slender, dark-skinned man, perhaps fifty years old, his nose long, his restless black eyes full of mirth and cunning. He is a member of the Episcopal church and a farmer.

He wears a black serge jacket with brass buttons and a white stock tied loosely at the neck. His hair is parted on the side and reaches to his shoulders. Dr. Brinton has seen the scars running up and down the chief's arms and back from his many knife fights with his half-brothers, and said he was known to be wild as a young man. His Mdewakanton name is Taoyatiduta, which means his people are red, but he prefers to be called Little Crow. He has six wives and is father to twenty-two children, seven of whom are living. He also has a double row of teeth. He visited Washington in 1858 to meet with President Buchanan in hope of negotiating a more favorable treaty for his people. He was a curiosity, and men flocked to his hotel to stare at him, but his attempts at statecraft had little effect. As the government has not kept its promises, many of the men in his band have lost confidence in him.

Three years ago, the Dakota chiefs were forced to sell yet more of their land to settle debts contrived by the traders. Dr. Brinton's brother encourages him to buy land along the north bank of the Minnesota, but my husband refuses to take Dakota land, although he has twice bought small parcels of town land at his brother's suggestion. Surely it is all Indian land.

The prairie around Yellow Medicine is fast disappearing on both sides of the river, from the town of Blue Earth to Mendota, and west to the Cottonwood River, bought for a half-dollar an acre by settlers from New England, Sweden, and Germany and by prosperous farmers in need of more land, or to herd cattle, or to build sawmills or trading posts. Some already settled families pack up and move a few miles to the west to start over again. Quakers, and backwoodsmen in raccoon caps, and uprooted Creoles, and Mormons arrive each day. It is easy to hate Indians if it means you can buy land cheap, with a few farm tools thrown in as enticements, usually a plow for fields yet to be cleared. I can hardly blame them, but I do. It is the promise of never-ending possibility that lures them. My husband minds them, too, but he takes the side of the Dakota in most things. Each of the settlers, each of the families, has stories to tell, and yet no one says a word. They are too harried, too restless to talk. Besides, no one is interested in their stories.

Dr. Brinton was called to the reservation this morning by the mother of a girl confined to one of the dark huts where menstruating women are kept to prevent defilement of the camp. She had been hemorrhaging for two days. He wished to remove the girl to the dispensary, fearing she had sepsis, but the elders would not allow it. He was not permitted to enter the enclosure, and he returned to the agency in low spirits and shut himself in the surgery. The girl, he said, will be dead by morning.

. . .

Even though I have now lived at Yellow Medicine for eleven months, I have yet to sleep through the night. To calm myself, I think of my favorite books, reminding myself of certain passages that make me laugh, or frighten me. Rather than light a lamp, I nurse Anne in the dark, made anxious by the sounds of the night and my apprehension of the prairie with its threat of endless time. I can smell the smoke of burning basswood as it drifts across the river from the camp, and the damp must of the cows in the dairy, and the stink of urine-soaked straw.

Each sound demands to be heard: the horses stamping in their sleep, the mice inching along the floorboards, the mysterious wood thrush digging in the porch railing for insects. My six canaries, envious of the night birds, peck restlessly at the shawl that covers their cage. Timber wolves range about the house, brushing against the front door, their yellow eyes widening and closing. Major Weems's black dog hears them, too, but he is locked in the warehouse, where he whines in fear.

I can hear James whispering companionably in his sleep, and Anne turning in her narrow cradle, yet another gift from my mother-in-law, with the date 1768 carved on its side, and my husband as he lurches into the dispensary in search of medicine to relieve his constipation. I stand on the porch, where I can see the fires, and the moon reflected in the black river. I sent away for a book about the planets and constellations, and I sometimes take a candle and the book outside with me to study the sky. This week, I was able to find Arcturus in the southeast and, just before dawn, Jupiter and a very faint Saturn, low in the sky.

Should my husband ever spend time with me, he would be surprised by the things that I know, not only the constellations, but Assyrian military tactics and the life of Governor DeWitt Clinton, although these are not, I admit, particularly scintillating subjects. We no longer pretend that we have chosen each other's company, knowing that we are bound together through circumstance and chance. Still, I do what I can to keep presentable. If I am plain, I can at least be clean. I hold my forearms over a fire to burn away the hair. I buff my nails with a chamois.

The Lost Wife

I am free of lice and other infestations. I change my petticoat once a week. I remove the calluses from my hands and feet with stones from the river. I pull the hair from my upper lip. I clean my ears with twigs of pussy willow. I brush my hair a hundred strokes every day. None of this does much for my looks, but why would it.

I sometimes wonder how much he knows. There are moments when I wish he would question me. A risky, even dangerous thought. At times he looks at me in disappointment, as if married life has not provided the compensations he'd hoped to find. At night, when he is finished treating his patients, his indifference increases with each sip of laudanum. His newspapers are in his lap, his feet in tapestry slippers as he reads week-old dispatches from the Army of the Potomac, sometimes made despondent and sometimes elated by news of the War. Even when he strikes me, it signifies nothing, not even boredom.

My behavior, however, is without implication, a necessity when one accumulates untruths, and yet I am tempted to tell him the truth, if only to provoke him. One's life can be precarious when one has invented it. As long as he believes me, I am in his power. If you tell lies, it is not, as you might think, you who has the advantage. I have noticed that most people who lie think that everyone else is lying, too, but I am not like that. I think that everyone but me is telling the truth.

When I am able to sleep for a few hours, I dream of a child. She is lame, with a tiny foot withered in the womb. I know her. Her name is Florence.

. . .

The Friendlies who have been baptized by Reverend Riggs at his farming community in Hazelwood are given Biblical names. I know two Saras, a Hagar, an Esther, a Ruth, and two men named Moses and Saul, although they only use their new names if the missionaries are nearby. Reverend Riggs is teaching them to read and write and to do figures, and has made a dictionary of the Sisseton dialect. They live in small brick houses built by the agency and wear homespun shirts and trousers. The women dress in cotton shifts made by the wives of the missionaries. They are taught to grow corn, wheat, and potatoes on the five acres of land allowed each of them by the government, and they are given two men's suits, a cow, a plow, and a churn in exchange for their promise to send their children to the mission school, to abstain from liquor, and to attend church. The men must cut their hair and keep it short, a requirement enforced by Mrs. Riggs, who cannot conceal the pleasure she takes in cutting their hair. It is unsettling to chance upon a shearing. Sometimes her hands tremble and she must put aside the scissors until she can calm herself. She told me that the mission's own small plot of wheat was grown from seeds found in the craw of a wild swan shot by Reverend Riggs, but I do not believe her.

I have begun to ride five miles through the woods to Sunday service at Reverend Riggs's church, sitting alongside the Friendlies on rough-hewn benches as they sing the hymns Reverend Riggs and his wife have taught them. Their favorite is sung to the tune of "Old Hundred." "Have mercy upon us, O Jehovah." I sing along with them, grateful for any spare mercy. On my way home, I vow to perform any number of kind acts each day. Beginning Monday. Or the next day, or the day after.

The Lost Wife

. . .

It is the season when the Dakota move to higher ground, leaving their winter quarters in the sheltered hollows near rivers and in woods where they are close to water and firewood. The different bands will gather at the Redwood Reservation, a narrow ten-mile strip on both sides of the river, each band in its own place, to hold councils and religious ceremonies and to plan war parties. Small family groups will hunt for game, a mystical undertaking requiring skill and the protection of the spirits, not a sport as Major Weems would have it. They will break camp in the fall after collecting their yearly annuity at the agency, paid in exchange for the sale of their land.

Whites like to think the Dakota have little attachment to the land, citing as evidence their seemingly random migration, but it is not true. The opposite is true. They have favorite hunting grounds and summer and winter camps to which they return each year with anticipation and even reverence. Or once returned. Much of it is no longer their land, and they now camp near trading posts and towns where they can buy food and provisions when there is no game.

Tonight my husband read a passage from Henry David Thoreau to me. The Jesuit priests who busied themselves burning Indians at the stake were astonished when their victims suggested more effective means of torture. "Being superior to physical suffering, it sometimes chanced that they were superior to any consolation which the missionaries could offer."

"I'm not sure that is true," he said.

.   .   .

Most days, I leave Anne with the Sisseton woman named Upahu, and James and I ride the chestnut mare named Snap into the woods. The Indian mounds are bright with prairie crocus and pasqueflower and a small bunched plant with flowers the color of dried blood. My husband says that in a mound in the Black-bird Hills, a chief was buried sitting upright on his live war pony. There are pale yellow violets and columbine, and viper's bugloss, poisonous to horses. The cedar trees are netted in grapevines, which the Sisseton women bring me to make wine. It is the sugar season, and I can hear them tapping the box elder trees for syrup. There is the smell of dry black earth.

Wild turkeys move across the plain, their heads bobbing above the grass, sometimes red and sometimes blue, depending on their mood. There are large noisy frogs, and inquisitive crows flying low over the trees. Meadowlarks make their nests in the grass, and I am afraid that Snap will step on them. There are hundreds of badger holes, and I worry, too, that she will stumble. Sometimes there is a sudden stillness, with only a faint murmur of wind, the clouds seeming not to move. Then there is more sky than I can understand. I keep moving so that it does not weigh on me.

Dr. Brinton has begun to teach James about fossils, showing him his finds and those specimens he buys from farmers. The Dakota give him worm casings and trilobites, and he gives them money in exchange, and food. James is sure he sees something on the prairie, and we dismount to make certain we have not overlooked the bones of a pterodactyl. Then there is a new smell of dry sage and mint and prairie dropseed, their scent released as we wade through the grass, the sharp stalks opening before us and closing behind us as we make a narrow path. Now and then we find the bleached spine of a buffalo.

On our way home, we stop at the Sisseton camp to eat spicy wild strawberries, and turnips, which the women have taught us to bite like apples. They fill one of their long pipes for me, tamping it with chips of red willow and the bark from the bear-berry shrub called kinnikinnick. The women like to spread rumors while we smoke, making each other laugh as the gossip grows more and more outlandish, and making me laugh, too. The men of mixed descent who speak English repeat everything the whites say, and as they often misconstrue or exaggerate our words, there are misunderstandings. The entire camp, even the men, lives for gossip. It is worse than Dexter Asylum.

The woman named Deep Lake is missing her nose, which, Dr. Brinton told me, was bitten from her face by her husband as a punishment for infidelity. It makes it hard to look at her. I am outraged each time I see her, but she accepts her punishment without blame. A betrayed woman is not allowed to bite off her husband's or her lover's nose, although she may stab his favorite horse to death.

I am mindful when I leave the camp to remove the feathers and amulets the women braid into James's hair while we smoke. Mrs. Flanagan asked me yesterday if James had lice. She herself has a goiter the size of an orange.

I live in two worlds now, spending the afternoon with the Sisseton women, smoking kinnikinnick and returning to the agency at dusk, a sleepy James cradled between the reins, to sit at the dining table to drink tea with Henrietta Weems from one of my mother-in-law's Wedgwood cups. I did not see it at first, but the Dakota women live in two worlds as well, working with me in the dark house, making blackberry cobbler and polishing mahogany sideboards, then returning to their tipis. I wonder what they think. They will never tell me. And I will never tell them. That is why it is two worlds, not one.

I discovered that the teachers at the school for Indian children feed them out of their own pocket, and I have been giving them food and James's outgrown clothes, shirts and pants too small for most of them, which they cut into strips to make skirts and neckcloths. The missionary Dr. Williston has a log church three miles from here, and some of the Christian Indians attend service there every Sunday. He, too, gives them what food he can spare. He has been in the valley for twenty-seven years.

.   .   .

The many newspapers we receive, some of them weeks old, are full of false reports, especially about the War. Only last week we read that General Joe Johnston, commander of the Confederate army, had been beheaded in a battle near Richmond, causing mostly jubilation, only to discover that he was alive, although he has been replaced by Robert E. Lee.

It is my birthday today. I am thirty-three years old, although I say that I am thirty. My husband gave me a pair of otter cuffs and a muff.

My life is a combination of fairy tale and newspaper report.

The Lost Wife

. . .

Those evenings when my husband is on the porch talking until dark with the chiefs, I like to steal into the dispensary to read the titles of his books. There is always something new, sent to him by booksellers in Boston and Philadelphia. It is a way to know him, as desperate as that sounds. Books by men with names hard to pronounce, as well as books like Yearsley's *On Throat Deafness* and *The Married Woman's Private Medical Companion* and Burton's *The Anatomy of Melancholy*, and I wonder, not for the first time, What is he doing here? I know why I am here, but what caused him to leave his comfortable life in Connecticut to work in the gold fields? To work unassisted and ill-equipped in Indian territory? I might understand if I thought he was content. It is whiskey and laudanum that soothe him for those few hours before he falls asleep. Like me, he has no religious convictions, rather a disdain for orthodoxy of any kind. He has no interest in the divine, other than what he can find in opium. I don't attend Reverend Riggs's mission because of a belief in the Almighty, but because it gives me an excuse to be alone for a few hours each Sunday. And I like the singing.

Before we left Shakopee, I made up a box of presents—a tin of licorice, some blue cotton stockings, a quill necklace made by one of the women, and a pair of doeskin gloves into which I tucked some money—and gave it to Mr. Spankle to mail to Florence when he traveled to Indianapolis. That way, I cannot be traced by the postmarks. I told him that post sent from Shakopee often takes months to arrive in the East, which is not true, but he did not question me. He was going to visit his dead wife's sister, unmarried at thirty-seven. They had never met, but she'd sent him a sketch she'd made of herself, looking handsome and perhaps twenty years old, which he persuaded himself was a true rendering. He has a very trusting nature. After all, he hired me. I will always be grateful for that.

I learned today that the young French wife of one of the carpenters, said to be his half-sister, disappeared during last night's storm. She fell into a malaise after the birth of their child a month ago and has several times been found wandering miles from the agency. Two nights ago, she hid the baby in a blanket and left the house with it, intending to walk to her birthplace in Little Canada, 130 miles to the north. Mdewakanton trackers have been sent after her.

.   .   .

Last night, I dreamed that the river rose more than thirty feet and Maddie's swollen white body, her eyes eaten by eels, floated to the surface from its grave of sand.

.   .   .

I invited Henrietta to ride with me and James, but her husband does not approve of women riding for pleasure. He says that he can smell the kinnikinnick smoke on me and has warned her against me. Although we are the same age, she seems younger, perhaps because she is smaller and more delicate. She is not someone you would think might take to the likes of me, and she didn't at first, but I let her see that I would cause her no harm, and she soon came to trust me. She is a good Catholic girl in the best sense, not like me, not even like Maddie, who pretended to say the Rosary every night. She likes Dr. Brinton, too, and sees that despite his occasional rages, he is a kind father.

Her daughter, Estelle, is nine months old. She was born early and is scrawny and vague of focus. Henrietta told me that she spent a month in bed after the child's birth and does not think she can safely bear another child. She spoke so hesitantly that I was not sure what she was trying to tell me. She said that her body had become hateful to her.

"The marital embrace," she said, looking at her feet. "It is something he requires."

"There is an herb called wormwood that makes a cleansing tea," I said. "Not to drink. You rinse yourself with it."

She nodded.

"It grows on the prairie. If you wish, I will ask the women to bring me some."

When I saw that I had not shocked or embarrassed her, I said, "There is another tea, made of tansy and rue, that will cause timely contractions in your womb. It is painful, but it achieves its purpose."

She nodded again.

.   .   .

This morning at breakfast, the house grew even darker than usual, and I thought the men had gathered at the windows, as they like to do. Suddenly, there was a banging, thudding sound on the roof and sides of the house. We ran onto the porch to find the sky black with migrating birds. The mountain ash were so laden with pigeons, talking without cease in their loud gurgling voices, that the branches began to crack and break. The birds looked as if they had suddenly been freed from a witch's spell, transported by their release and trembling with joy.

The agency men abandoned their work to swing at the birds with hoes and shovels, and Major Weems, who boasts that he can bring down thirty pigeons with a single shot, ran into the yard, firing his shotgun into the air. Birds fell onto our heads from the trees and the sky, and mounted in quivering piles at our feet. There will be so many dead pigeons in the yard tonight that even the wolves will grow sick of them.

Some of the Irishmen fell to their knees to pray. Mr. Schneider, one of the surveyors from St. Paul, dropped his sextant in alarm. Dr. Brinton, who has made a study of pigeon migrations, said the birds were on their way to their nesting spot in the oak barrens of northern Minnesota, an area that covers almost a thousand square miles. I did not want to watch the slaughter and went inside with Anne. James refused to go with us, spinning in circles beneath the falling birds.

. . .

Dr. Brinton told me that the French girl's shoes and a baby's blanket were found by the trackers ten miles from the agency.

. . .

The Lost Wife

I read in the St. Anthony newspaper that Mr. Lincoln has requested that Governor Ramsey send him an additional fifty thousand Minnesota volunteers. He also ordered that any slave who volunteers for military labor be given his freedom. Many in the army object to this.

There is a Negro here named Thomas Quigley who looks after the stock, and my husband told him of this new order. Thomas says he is happy to labor at the agency, but does not want to labor for Lincoln and be free and dead.

.   .   .

To my surprise, Dr. Brinton asked me to visit with him in his dispensary tonight. One of the traders lost a finger in a knife fight with a Canadian trapper, and there was a pile of bloodstained gauze and cotton on the examining table. Also a torn otter pelt, which I assumed had something to do with their quarrel.

He sat in his desk chair, his long legs stretched before him, and I sat on a stool like a patient waiting to be examined. Perhaps I was. I noticed a hole in the sole of one of his boots. His gold watch fob was missing. He no longer tends to his appearance as he once did. No more cambric neckerchiefs, no more polka-dot socks.

He said he tries not to let it bother him, but the thought of certain food sometimes keeps him awake at night. He asked me what food and drink I most missed. When I smiled, he shook his head and said, "I am utterly serious, and I ask that you answer with equal gravity."

"Yes, yes, I will," I said, "but you go first. You have been thinking about it and are ready with your list."

"Yes," he said, and he, too, smiled. "Mandarin oranges. The occasional Dover sole. Figs. Connecticut corn, not this pig corn. Pineapple upside-down cake. Your more delicate lettuces."

Now I was laughing.

"Your turn," he said.

"Your tastes are rather refined," I said. "Mine are more Irish. Curds. Porter. Colcannon. Tomatoes."

"Are tomatoes Irish?" he asked. "I'd have thought not."

"Let me try again," I said. "Cider."

"I can get you cider," he said.

He has never been so nice to me.

. . .

There was meant to be a wedding at the agency this afternoon between one of the young Sisseton women who looks after the hens and an otter hunter from Mankato. In preparation, I made a cherry cake, and the blacksmith killed twenty-four of the rattlesnakes living in holes in the yard. We waited for hours in the heat, the girl weeping, but the man did not appear. Later, we learned he was so drunk he could not stand. It is not known if the wedding will now take place, although the bride is willing.

I have been teaching James his letters, the Sisseton children watching from the porch, silent for once. When I saw that he was showing them how to form the letters, drawing in the dirt with a stick, I invited them inside. Now they all sit at the dining room table, learning to write the alphabet. Some of them are quicker at it than James. When we are finished, there is tea and corn bread.

.   .   .

I left the house alone this afternoon, walking north for an hour in the hope of finding someone who might have seen the French girl and her baby. I stopped at the farm of a Wahpeton chief named John Otherday and spoke to a young white couple who looked like runaways themselves, barely in their teens and living in a dilapidated cabin on his farm, but they had not seen the girl or her child. John Otherday said there was a pack of wolves living in a den not far from his farm. He said to be sure I was home by dark, as he saw them last night near his stock pen. Or better still, I thought, home by twilight, the hour of the wolf, as my mother liked to say.

I continued walking. A mysterious elation began to overtake me, seeming to grow the farther I was from home. I felt the world pressing against me and I began to tremble. The air, flattened and still, held me tightly. The enormity of it, the prairie and the sky and the rushing rivers, no longer frighten me, but fill me with joy. Such beauty! I felt a sudden deep thrill of gratitude, but to whom? When it began to alarm me, I turned around.

.   .   .

It will soon be the month the Santee call the Moon of the Ripening Chokecherries, the time when they break their yearlings and two-year-old ponies, and the women repair their tipis. This morning, men from the camp came to borrow our washtubs. They use them to mix clay to make war paint. I could see Major Weems watching from the window of his office, and I said yes, they could have the washtubs.

French trappers, many of them of mixed descent, arrived a few hours later, driving their Red River carts past the agency on their way from Fort Garry in Winnipeg south to St. Anthony. They are rough-looking, excitable men, eager to take offense, dressed in enormous beaver hats, and pelts bound with silk sashes. Their wild hair hangs down their backs and across their chests. The heavily laden carts have two enormous wooden wheels which leave deep ruts in the road. James likes to play in the ruts, his map turtle, caught for him by one of the Sisseton boys, struggling to climb one of the dusty furrows only to slide to the bottom before it can reach the top. I cannot bear to watch it. The trappers will camp at the edge of the plain tonight, where they will play music and jig until dawn, their black silhouettes leaping and tumbling around their fires. I've been anticipating their coming all day. I'd like to dance with them.

Tonight, when my husband came to bed with his potion of cardamom and brandy and green beetle, he stopped upon seeing my expression and said that he would gladly forgo the ritual were it not that he suffers from an affliction called "Thompson's disease," which is caused by an excess of sentiment. He does not see how he can be blamed for that. "No," I said, "except that you are lying. You have made up Thompson's disease." Which is when he threw the bowl against the wall and slapped me. He did not mix a new solution, and it was worth a sore jaw for that.

This morning, there was a tremendous storm. I could smell it as it approached, and then I heard the slow plump drops, now here, now there, as they bounced on the dry ground, and then more drops, coming faster and faster, until the roof clattered with a sound like rifle shots.

.   .   .

Mr. Flanagan, the blacksmith, wrote a barely legible, supposedly anonymous letter to Major Weems, complaining that Thomas Quigley is a runaway slave. He wants to tie him up and take him to St. Paul, where there is a bounty for captured slaves. I heard this from Henrietta and told my husband, who went to see Major Weems in his office. He told him that Thomas is a free man and that he has seen the papers proving him so. I have no idea what papers he is talking about, but the blacksmith has sent no more letters.

.   .   .

I have become a member of a lending library in Philadelphia. My third parcel of books arrived today, among them *Malaeska: The Indian Wife of the White Hunter,* by Mrs. Ann S. Stephens. It is a very popular book, and I have been on the waiting list for five months. I also borrowed a book called *Plots of the Great*

Operas, which I hope will expand my mind. The other books are for pleasure. *The Black Tulip* and *David Copperfield,* and Mrs. G. M. Flanders's book, *The Ebony Idol,* which I will read first. I borrowed books for James as well. I am teaching him to read. *Tom Thumb's Picture Alphabet* and *A Little Book for Little People.*

I also subscribe to certain ladies' illustrated magazines, in part so that I, too, receive mail.

July 1862

LAST MONTH, MAJOR WEEMS and my husband visited the Dakota living near Big Stone Lake to ask them not to come to the agency until Major Weems sends word, as their annuity will be late this year. Despite this request, they arrived today, camping a mile away. They are running out of food, and game is scarce thanks to the fires set by farmers to clear the land. Last winter, there was no forage because of an unusual amount of snow, and they were forced to slaughter their few pigs and cattle. The Friendlies are given generous amounts of food and other provisions all year long, but they will sell their crops only to the traders and refuse to feed their relatives.

As their annuity has not arrived, the chiefs hope to be given food, an arrangement my husband says is clearly stated in their treaty. Today when the men, eager to leave for their summer grounds, asked Major Weems for food, he told them to return in three weeks, when the money will surely be here. He turned away angrily when he saw me watching him and pushed past me, shouting that he will pay them when the gold arrives. "What are they moaning about?" he asked. "They sell land they themselves claim they don't own. It seems it's the Great Spirit we should be paying."

Yesterday, while celebrating the Fourth of July with the Weems family and the agency workers, dancing to fiddle music as we drank blackberry wine, ten Dakota men approached the agency on horseback to ask that Major Weems unlock the warehouse and give them food. When he refused to do so, some of the workmen ran to hide in the jail, leaving behind their women and children, and Mrs. Flanagan shouted at the braves to leave at once or she'd see them horsewhipped. They looked at her without expression, perhaps because she spoke in English.

I took Henrietta's hand and began to dance, gesturing to the fiddler to keep playing as I drew the children into a circle, the workers' dogs joining us with excited yips and leaps. The braves stared at us in astonishment, commenting to one another on our performance. Major Weems watched for a minute or two, then spat in the dirt and motioned to the fiddler to stop playing.

I caught my breath and gestured to the men to dismount and follow me onto the porch, where I offered them strawberry ice cream, explaining in Dakota that we were dancing in happiness, not in preparation for war. My husband does not celebrate the Fourth of July, as he agrees with the abolitionist Douglass that it is a day of mourning, not rejoicing, but he came from the dispensary when he heard us and helped to cut the ice cream into slices. I could see that for once he was pleased with me. Later, I made him laugh when I said, "Have you noticed that they really do say, 'How'? I thought it was only in dime novels."

"I believe they fancy you," he said with a smile. I looked at him in surprise, but he turned away, licking the last of the ice cream from a spoon.

.　.　.

The last day of the July ritual known as the Gaze at the Sun Suspended will be held this afternoon. There has been dancing and chanting and the sound of drums and whistles for the last eight days. No one from the camp has appeared at the agency in more than a week. I am surprised by how much I depend on them, not because of the work they do, but because of their company.

Dr. Brinton sits on the porch in a rocker, a spyglass in his lap. A jug of whiskey and a glass are on a table next to him, and his brown bottle of laudanum. The men perform the ceremony to thank the sun god for granting each of them a favor, perhaps in battle or for sparing the life of a sick child. They pierce their chests with hooks attached by rawhide ropes to a central hollow post and dance until they reach a state of delirium. Beds of sage are prepared for them on which to rest during pauses in the dance, and where attendants and friends can cleanse their wounds. The men who complete the ritual and who receive a vision are deemed shamans and afforded the highest honor and respect. Dr. Brinton will watch them through the night. "Would it were so easy," he said mysteriously.

.　.　.

Sometimes I stand in the alcove behind the dispensary stairs to listen to my husband and Major Weems while they play cards, which is how I know what my husband is thinking. He says that he wishes he could join the Union Army. He would go as a surgeon. Although he has done only a few amputations in his life, most of the deaths in the War, he says, are from disease. "One of my friends from medical school has joined the Confederacy. He is from Richmond. I was once engaged to his sister."

"Is that so?" Major Weems asked. "My deal?"

"I could be of use. The first regiment of Minnesota Volunteers left St. Paul only last week. Just in time to fight at Bull Run."

"You could make some money," Weems said. "You don't even have to go. Examining doctors are paid by the recruit."

"Not go?" my husband asked in surprise. "Unfortunately, they don't favor men, even doctors, who are more than six foot three. Tall men are thought to be incapable of enduring fatigue."

"Ha," said Major Weems.

.   .   .

They have changed toward us, unwilling to share a pipe or to gossip, eager to be away, silent and ill at ease. They no longer stand at the windows to watch us. When I see them in the yard, they walk past without meeting my glance or greeting me. They, too, have heard the rumors that because of the War, there will be no annuity this year.

Last week, Major Weems requested that a company of soldiers from Fort Ridgely, forty miles to the southeast, be sent to the agency. A young lieutenant named Costello arrived today with one hundred men. Their haphazard uniforms looked old and incomplete, too tight under the arms and in the seat, or too large. Some of them were wearing Mexican sombreros, and I wondered if proper uniforms were saved for the Union soldiers fighting in the War. The children and I watched as they erected four rows of tents behind the warehouse and posted pickets. To my surprise, Lieutenant Costello speaks Dakota.

. . .

Five thousand Dakota have gathered in the valley to beg for food. Hundreds of men on horseback and in wagons wait in the field behind the agency, their thin legs pressed against the protruding ribs of their ponies.

Lieutenant Costello asked to see Major Weems, but the major had disappeared. He called the chiefs into the yard and, to my relief, opened the warehouse, ordering his men to stand at arms as the agency workmen rolled out barrels of flour and corn and pork. I wondered if it was because his men were outnumbered and he feared for our safety.

He gave them only enough food to keep their people alive for another week. They trembled with rage, their faces pinched with bitterness. I thought that if Lieutenant Costello's strategy was to keep them weak and dependent, it was a dangerous one. He knows nothing about the Sioux, despite the fact that my husband tells me he has a Sisseton wife with whom he lives openly.

There was a growing tightness in the air as the men silently loaded the barrels onto their wagons. As they left, I heard them singing in Dakota, "The old men so few, they are not worth counting. I myself am the last living. A hard time I am having."

They now will be forced to buy food on credit from the traders, further diminishing the amount of money owed them by the government. The traders will present them with blank vouchers or receipts scribbled with random numbers, sometimes even pages of newsprint, meant to show how much they have spent at the trading posts. The government pays each man nine dollars a year, scant recompense for the sale of twenty-four million acres of land. When the traders see that any charges will be in excess of a man's annuity, they refuse him credit. Last year, I saw one of the men swallow the coins given him rather than pay the traders. I said nothing, but I was glad.

The white men use the money meant for the Dakota for their own wages, as well as their building and farming projects. They seek their posts in expectation of gain and they are not disappointed. Mr. Ramsey, superintendent of Indian affairs and later territorial governor, took $65,000, and his secretary $55,000, of the nearly half million dollars promised the tribes in 1851. General Henry Sibley, a former fur trader and first governor of the state of Minnesota, awarded himself $145,000 of one year's annuity, which he claimed was owed him for his part in negotiating the treaty.

·   ·   ·

It is now the thirtieth of July, and the money that is owed the Dakota still has not arrived. The men are too weak and sick to hunt. They have slaughtered their few remaining cows and hogs, and finished the flour and corn that Lieutenant Costello gave them, eating the corn raw like cattle. They scavenge for old bones to cut in pieces, holding them to the fire to kill the worms and maggots, then boil them to drink the broth. Sometimes they will trap a squirrel. They eat any wild birds they can catch, and muskrats. They eat the bark of trees and the roots of a grass that grows along the river, and wood sorrel and alum bulbs. They eat old beaver-skin rugs, singeing away the hair and cutting the pelts into strips. They eat my roses. They eat the ears of their horses. The old women tell me it is their job to search for any small caches of beans hidden by field mice. Many have died of starvation and disease.

I do what I can, taking them flour and meat from our own stores and vegetables from the garden, but their need is inexhaustible, and Major Weems has threatened me with, of all things, insubordination. Although we have barrels of crackers and cheese and salted fish, Dr. Brinton will not allow me to dispense them. We have no more corn, and our supply of flour is growing low.

He works through the night, treating the children. They suffer from measles and typhus, as well as acute diarrhea from eating green fruit. Several have died after chewing the flowers of the white camas plant. There is so much diarrhea in camp that the tipis must be moved every few days.

.　.　.

Two Sisseton arrived at the agency this morning to tell Lieutenant Costello—they will no longer parley with Weems—that warriors would soon be arriving to fire a salute in gratitude for his help. Dr. Brinton sent me word of this as I was working in the garden with Henrietta, and we took the children into the house, not wanting them to be frightened by the noise.

An hour later, I saw a thousand warriors in war paint coming across the plain, singing and firing their guns. As they reached the agency, the braves jumped from their ponies and ran to the warehouse, where they began to hack at the doors with their spears. Little Crow and three of his men came up the porch steps and into the house, shouting and swinging their blankets as they demanded I give them an ax. James was playing on the floor with Jacob and looked up with a smile when he saw them. Henrietta, both Anne and her own baby in her arms, stood behind me.

Little Crow's war bonnet reached the low ceiling of the hall. He was no longer dressed in trousers and a gingham shirt, but wore a breechcloth and quilled leggings decorated with tufts of hair, and a necklace of bear claws. He had painted a red hand across his mouth and I could smell the paint. I had taken hold of a pistol when I first saw them in the yard and hid it in the folds of my skirt. When I saw that they meant us no harm, I slipped the gun behind a sofa cushion and showed them the ax kept under the back stairs.

Lieutenant Costello ordered the soldiers to strip away what was left of the doors, gesturing to the braves to take what food they could carry. The men dragged barrels of flour and corn from the warehouse and loaded them onto their wagons. As they pushed their way past him, Costello shouted that he would give them more food in the morning as well as hold a council, provided they leave the agency.

I am not sure he has the authority to make such demands, but it hardly mattered. Major Weems had disappeared. I noticed that several of the soldiers had pissed their pants. The hot air was filled with dust and there was the smell of horses and sweat. Dr. Brinton emerged from the dispensary in his white coat, holding an excited James by the hand and what looked like a scalpel in his other hand, and stood on the porch with me and Henrietta.

As Little Crow mounted his pony, he laughed and waved the ax at me, his many teeth seeming to spill from his mouth. When the braves rode away, the soldiers yelled threats at them and fired their own rifles into the air. It was difficult to hear, but as Dr. Brinton took Anne from my arms, he said, "Have you lost your mind, wife?"

Later that evening, I overheard Major Weems tell Mr. Gamp, a trader who owns stores at both the Lower and Upper Agencies, that Lieutenant Costello had earlier sent a message to Fort Ridgely requesting more men. Mr. Gamp wears a wig of badger pelts with a white stripe across the top of his head, which he must consider distinguished, as he could have the pelts without the stripe. Lieutenant Costello asked Mr. Gamp if he would give the Indians some of his own stock when they returned in the morning, but Mr. Gamp walked out of the room, saying, "If the Dakota are so hungry, they can eat grass. Or their own dung, if they prefer."

. . .

This morning, a Captain Marsh arrived from the fort with a company of soldiers and ordered Weems to dispense more food to the Sioux. The captian told Mr. Gamp that he would be arrested if he caused any unrest. More than one hundred barrels of flour and thirty barrels of pork were given to the men when they arrived an hour later, and Captain Marsh returned this afternoon to Fort Ridgely, saluting James as he left the yard.

.   .   .

I asked my husband before he escaped upstairs tonight if there was news of the War. He said that the Battle of Bull Run had been a ruinous defeat, causing three thousand Federal casualties. It was a shock to the North, which had anticipated a short war. The First Minnesota was one of the last regiments to leave the field, with forty-nine killed and thirty-four missing. Men who were not injured stole the ambulances to flee to Washington, leaving behind the wounded and dying. Lincoln has called for 300,000 volunteers for McClellan's Army of the Potomac.

I noticed that one of the books recently arrived from his bookseller in Philadelphia is *A Manual of Military Surgery*. It was open to Chapter VI, "Amputations and Resections."

August 1862

THERE ARE RUMORS THAT the Dakota are going to attack the agency, and my husband has decided to send me and the children to Redwood Falls, where he thinks it best we spend the night before continuing to Fort Ridgely. He claimed he did not believe the rumors, which made no sense to me. When I questioned why, if he did not believe the rumors, he wished us to leave, he said that the Dakota had no power. Their power is imaginary, he said. Which made even less sense. "We have been killing them since the beginning," he said. "A less tolerant people would have taken their revenge years ago." His speech was muddled, which made me think he had been drinking laudanum.

"Imaginary power is dangerous, too," I said. "There is no end to it."

I didn't want to leave, but he had made up his mind. I am usually able to have my way, which is one benefit of his inattention, but he was adamant. We are to leave in the morning. Rather than wait for a stagecoach that is due later in the week, he arranged for a clerk named Manse Hawkins to take us in exchange for the use of a wagon, which Manse needs to transport two young shoats to the fort.

I knew that Major Weems left Yellow Medicine earlier in

the week to deliver a small party of Union recruits called the Renville Rangers to Fort Snelling, and I asked if Henrietta and her children could come with us in the wagon. "Surely Major Weems will want them to be safe."

"Major Weems knows how to take care of his family," he said, as if to suggest I was impugning his judgment, which was just what I was doing. "Besides, there is no room for them."

"But we can take two wagons," I said.

"Major Weems has taken the rest of the wagons to Fort Snelling, in hope of returning with provisions."

I packed slowly, ignoring my husband's insistence that I take nothing with me, throwing the boy's harmonica, a book of crochet patterns, *David Copperfield,* and six silver forks into a basket. I covered the birdcage and bound it tightly. I wrapped James's biscuit tin containing the mosasaur tooth he found with his father, and Anne's wicker chair, and they were loaded onto the wagon with three baskets of plums and four casks of water. As I folded a set of napkins sent last Christmas by Dr. Brinton's mother, I did for an instant wonder if he was right and if I had lost my mind, but quickly dismissed the thought and made a pile of ladies' magazines to take with me. That is when I noticed that my hands were shaking.

I gathered the presents I'd put aside for Florence—a gingham sunbonnet, a bolero of Irish lace made by the wife of one of the carpenters, and what money I had on hand—and made a small parcel to give to anyone at the fort who would be traveling. There was always someone on his way somewhere who would mail it for me. It is unlikely after all this time that Ank is looking for me, but I am still careful to hide my whereabouts.

The Lost Wife

. . .

I awoke at dawn and put on my plaid skirt and bodice, and my gray leather boots. I looked for Upahu to say goodbye, but she had disappeared, which was unusual. Henrietta came to the house, Estelle in her arms, to kiss me goodbye. She said that we would not be gone long and that she would tend the garden while I was away. I was reluctant to leave her, aware of something in the air that frightened me, perhaps my husband's bad nerves.

I climbed into the wagon. My husband handed Anne to me and helped us onto the plank seat. James squeezed himself between the crate holding the shoats and the baskets of plums, his turtle in a burlap sack. The pigs followed him with their eyes, black beneath their pale lashes.

It was shortly after three when we at last left. Manse was oddly gay, laughing at everything I said in a loud, unrestrained voice, helpless with glee. Picking food from his discolored teeth with a goose quill, he said that the Federals would catch him sooner or later, and I wondered if he was a deserter. His hair was long, which is perhaps why I had not earlier noticed that he was missing an ear.

The dust rose from the road as we rattled along, coating our hands and faces, and making James sneeze. The Redwood River was on our left, and on our other side were the villages of three of the chiefs, including the tipis of Little Crow's band. I could see his brick house, built for him by the government. There were no other wagons on the road, and no people, Indian or white, which surprised me. No animals. I asked Manse if he had a gun, and he said, "Good Christ, lady, who do you think I am?"

About ten miles from the agency, he stopped the wagon to beg some chewing tobacco of Flem Welks, a trader who kept a small store near the river. Mr. Welks is said to be on too familiar terms with one of his mules, a story which Major Weems delights in repeating. He peered at us from behind his door and, when he saw that it was Manse, stepped into the light, his hand shading his eyes. In his other hand he held a shotgun. He was the first person we'd seen since leaving the agency. He said four boys from the Rice Creek band had killed some settlers that morning in Acton, twenty miles to the north. It seems they challenged a white farmer to a shooting contest, then shot him and his wife and three other men. The Mdewakanton and Sisseton bands were meeting to decide whether they would go to war or flee to the west. "The settlers are running," he said.

When I told Manse to turn around, he said he would never take me anywhere again. He had not known I was such a troublesome woman. Mrs. Flanagan had warned him, and he wished he'd listened to her. He said we were only twenty miles from Redwood Falls and I'd best keep my thoughts to myself for the rest of the trip. We would be there in three hours.

"I don't want you to take me anywhere, now or ever," I said.

Mr. Welks said, "You'd best quit jabbering and keep moving. I'm running, too." He tossed Manse a wad of tobacco and bolted the door of his store.

We had gone another six miles when I saw a black cloud moving swiftly toward us. I thought it might be the pigeons passing through, but it was not that time of year. Then I began to smell smoke. Sparks were landing in the grass, fanned by a sudden hot wind, and my eyes began to smart. I knew that we were near Bibb Zucker's farm, and I asked Manse if we could stop there. To my surprise, he said he was inclined to oblige me, but only that once. As we turned into the yard, I saw that it was deserted. It was time for milking, time to start a fire in the kitchen and to feed the pigs, but there was no one, no men or women or children, no horses or mules, not even a dog. An uneven row of men's hats hung from nails on the side of the house, as if they hadn't had time to grab them.

"Perhaps Mr. Gamp's sawmill is on fire and it has spread to the prairie," I said. "One of those fires that moves fast. That is why no one is here."

"You shut up," Manse said, moaning through his teeth.

Two men were coming through the grass. I told Manse to hold his gun where they could see it.

"What gun?" he said, as the men reached the wagon.

"Whip the horse," I said as he let the reins fall from his hands.

"I can't never get the straight of nothing," he said with a sob.

One of the men, tall and thin, dressed in a blue calico shirt and cotton trousers, was known to me from Shakopee, where his mother, Talutah, had helped me with the children. He asked if I was the wife of the doctor and if his mother had once worked for me, and I nodded. His name was Chaska. I knew that his father and younger brother had been killed years earlier in a raid by the Ojibwe. He'd been one of the young Christian Indians at Reverend Hinman's mission school. I had not seen him in two years, but I remembered him very well. He had a small scar, perhaps an inch and a half long, running from the right side of his mouth toward his ear. It was hard not to notice it, especially as it seemed to change color in different light. He was a favorite among the white women because of his quiet nature and because of a certain innocent beauty. He was a favorite, too, of Reverend Hinman, who arranged for him to do odd jobs for the women. He later married a girl from the Wahpekute band and they left Shakopee, although I later heard that she drowned. He was no longer the slender boy who milked cows for white ladies, but thicker and stronger. More solemn, with a certain disdainful gravity, as if someone or something had let him down along the way.

The other man was dressed in buckskin and carried a pistol. Without warning, he fired at Manse, striking him in the shoulder. Manse fell sideways into my lap, pinning Anne to my chest. James stood in alarm, his face covered with blood. I thought for a moment he, too, had been shot and pulled him to me, but it was Manse's blood. The man shot Manse again, and he flew from the wagon, landing in a bank of goldenrod. As he fell, the mare began to bolt, and Chaska ran after her, catching the reins in time. As he climbed onto the wagon, he said that if I spoke or looked at his companion, whom he called Hepan, the man would kill me and the children. He said Hepan was drunk. I told Chaska I would kill my children myself, rather than let Hepan touch them, and he gestured to me to be still.

Manse was still alive, his legs bucking up and down. Hepan ran to the bank and kicked him in rage, then shot him again and his legs stopped twitching. He came to the side of the wagon where I crouched with the children, and said that it was time to kill them, as they would be nothing but trouble. Chaska took hold of his arm and told him he could have Manse's shoats, but he would take the children. He told him I was the wife of Dr. Brinton and reminded him of the Dakota men whose lives my husband had saved.

They argued for what seemed a long time, but perhaps wasn't long at all. I was sick to my stomach and vomited over the side of the wagon. Chaska twice knocked the pistol from Hepan's hand. At last they seemed to agree, and Chaska turned the wagon as Hepan climbed into the back, throwing over the side James's turtle and all the bundles except for my trunk and the canaries and Manse's shoats. He quickly fell asleep, wrapped in a shawl he pulled from the trunk. It all seemed very orderly and reasonable, the way events in dreams seem to make sense. I could hear my own breathing with unusual clarity, and my heartbeat, and the harsh cries of the blackbirds as they fled the smoke, and the grunts of the shoats, and the frogs on the riverbank. I could feel Anne's breath on my cheek and James's hand on my wrist.

Chaska said that Chief Little Crow's encampment was not far, and we would be safe there, as Dr. Brinton had treated Little Crow once when he had measles and another time when he had been wounded in a fight with the Ojibwe. As we left the road to the Upper Agency, I saw the body of the trader, Mr. Gamp. He was dead, a scythe in his chest. His badger wig was gone. Clumps of grass had been stuffed in his mouth. A plank lay across his legs, on which the words "Feed your own women and children grass" had been scrawled. My first thought was that it must have been written by one of the Friendlies, as only they among the Dakota know how to write.

It was dark when we reached the village. There was the smell of gunpowder and horses and roasting meat. Dozens of excited dogs raced through the camp. I saw plows and two-handed saws and a mandolin, and splintered trunks, one with what looked like clerical vestments spilling over the sides. There were feather beds, some of them ripped apart, their feathers floating in the thick air, and a child's painted rocker. Barrels of whiskey, and bushels of potatoes and corn, and rashers of bacon, and sides of venison, and live cows stumbling in fear. Women fought over sacks of flour and sugar, grabbing what they could carry and hurrying to their tipis. Children squatted on the ground to eat the sugar and flour that had spilled, their mouths white with caked flour as they fought off the dogs. There was death now, but there was food.

Then I saw the white women and children, some of them in torn clothing, others with their breasts uncovered and blood running down their legs, pushed along by braves carrying toma-hawks and rifles. There were men prisoners, too, many of them of mixed descent. They looked as if they did not know where they were or how they came to be there. Children screamed as they were pulled from their mother's arms, the women strug-gling to keep hold of them until the braves struck them with the butts of their guns and they fell to the ground. The warriors were drunk, laughing as they fired their guns in the air, and sing-ing and dancing. One of the men wore Mr. Gamp's wig. Another carried my lime-green parasol.

Chaska's mother began to cry when she saw us, hiding Anne and me under a blanket as she took James from my arms and pulled us into her tipi. Her name is Talutah. She reminded me that she had worked for me in Shakopee, where she had cared for

Anne when she was born, and I told her that I remembered her very well, her kindness, and her affection for James.

Hepan followed us to the back of the tipi and began to throw corncobs at us, which made James laugh until I hushed him. Hepan said the men were waiting until morning to kill the captive women and their children. Talutah whispered that he was married to Chaska's half-sister Wenonah, the woman sitting near the fire. Hepan is a Rice Creek Indian, she said, but we belong to one band and one family. When I asked how the children and I would be killed, Hepan's wife smiled and stabbed at her breast. She told me to remove my hoop, as she wants to use it to dry scalps.

Chaska dragged my trunk into the tipi, and Wenonah crawled past the fire to go through it. She wrapped one of my embroidered shifts around her shoulders and wound a pair of stockings around her waist. Her face was heavily tattooed and she looked like a demon.

I was unable to eat, but James was hungry and drank the tea that Talutah made for him. I wrapped the children in rugs and lay next to them, crooning to them until I, too, fell into a dazed and mindless sleep.

.   .   .

It is the eighteenth of August. The first day of our captivity.

Chaska no longer wears white men's clothes. It seems that Snap now belongs to him. I asked if he knew what had happened to my husband and to Henrietta and her children. The Dakota are killing everyone across the river and as far north as Hutchinson, he said.

We are accidental captives, I said to myself. They did not set out to capture us. "We are accidental captives," I said aloud, but he did not answer me. I know that I will not be able to escape with two small children. They know it, too. I will make James memorize his father's name in case I am killed. I will speak in Dakota, except when I have something to say to Talutah that I don't want the others or the children to understand.

I sat in the dim light of the tipi, the children on my lap, my skirt damp with urine. Talutah gave us bacon, corn bread with sugar, and broth. I filled my mouth with one hand while I fed the children with the other, crumbs of corn bread falling into Anne's hair. As I reached for another piece of bacon, it came to me that we were eating food looted from the farms. Farms where men and women and children lay dead. I tried to spit out the food, but I couldn't. I was hungry. It was only when I found James playing with a handful of tiny beaks that I realized my canaries had gone into the broth.

Talutah removed my skirt and bodice and dressed me in an elk-skin skirt and leggings. Anne was wrapped in skins and bound to a cradle board. James was dressed in leggings and a long rawhide shirt, and we were given moccasins. Chaska watched in silence while Talutah parted my hair in the middle and smoothed it with bear fat before braiding it. She rubbed dirt on my face and into James's hair.

.   .   .

Last night, I heard a woman pleading to be killed. I crawled to the door of the tipi to look outside. Two braves wearing a strip of white cloth around their heads were dragging a naked white girl into an enclosure made of freshly cut boughs. There was a pile of women's clothing on the ground and an unhitched oxcart with what looked like pale arms and legs hanging over the sides. As I hurried to the back of the tipi, Wenonah grabbed hold of my ankle. Soon, she whispered. Your turn will be soon. I put my hands over my ears, but I could still hear the screams. After a while, there was laughter, then silence.

This morning, a young white girl crawled into the tipi. The children were asleep. Chaska and Hepan were not there, and Talutah and Wenonah had gone to the river to bathe. I offered the girl what remained of my breakfast of flatbread and tea, but she would not take it. She seemed feverish, and there was a rotten smell about her. Her skirt was stained with blood. When I moved closer to her, she shouted, "Don't touch me!" waking the children, who stared at her in fright. She wanted to know why we had buffalo rugs to sleep on, while she is dragged into the leaf hut two and three times a night.

I said Talutah had told me that if we wore Indian clothes and did not complain or try to escape, and, most of all, if I made myself useful, my children and I would not be harmed. She began to laugh, spreading her legs so that I could see the lesions on her labia and the streaks of dried blood on her thighs. I said there were herbs and teas that would help her to heal and I would bring them to her. I told her that I would help her to escape, but she paid me no mind, clawing at her cheeks until the sides of her face began to bleed. She crawled to the door of the tipi and pushed her way outside, her skirt around her hips.

Now there is the sound of drums and singing as Little Crow and his warriors prepare to attack the fort. I was put to work pounding meat for the men to take with them. My hands shook so badly that I worked very slowly, causing one of the women to shout that I am useless.

I was surprised to see that Chaska was going with them. I had not expected it. You might even call it a miscalculation. He is my good Indian, in part because he speaks English and once wore serge trousers rather than a breechcloth and had been to the mission school, where he learned the Ten Commandments, but mainly because he has kept me and my children alive. I wanted to tell him that they cannot win, but he knows that. It matters little what crimes have been committed against the Dakota; this uprising will always be thought more horrific than anything the whites have done to them.

. . .

Little Crow and his army returned near dawn. I could hear drumming and the shouts of the women as they learned of their dead, and the chants of the medicine men as they tended the wounded. The warriors sang, "Here is your son, his spirit and body are now one." Some of the men fell to the ground, where they slept in exhaustion. Hepan came into the tipi, boasting that hundreds of soldiers had been killed at the fort, with only a few Dakota dead, but I did not believe him.

The Lost Wife

Tonight, when I could not sleep, I tried to imagine how in only a few hours my husband's day would begin. He will eat his breakfast of oatmeal and berries and drink a glass of buttermilk, although not before meeting with the Sisseton trackers, whom he will invite to share his food, despite knowing that they will refuse. He has already located the Canadian trapper who lives on a flatboat on the river and speaks Dakota, who is said to know the country better than anyone, even the Santee, and who will ride with them. He has money in case he needs to pay a ransom. He will clean his gun, last used a year ago to frighten the wolves from the porch. He will pack a small rucksack, as he will need to travel lightly. He will draw a map. He will leave a letter for his brother in case he does not return. And then he will come for us.

.　.　.

It is the twenty-second of August. The fifth day of our captivity.

Last night, when I crawled outside to urinate, I saw a cart loaded with what looked like the bodies of women captives, their hair visible beneath the rugs thrown over them. I pulled one of the rugs from the cart, but it was only buffalo hair.

The white captives roam about the camp at night. They sometimes stop at Chaska's tipi to ask me to walk with them, but I cannot leave the children. Some of the men captives are with them. I encourage them to run away, especially the young girls, but they are too afraid, knowing the men will kill them if they are caught.

I no longer have any milk. Talutah makes a drink for Anne

by beating walnut kernels with cornmeal and water, and then boiling it in a skin bag. After I feed Anne, she gives what is left to James. He says it is better than cows' milk.

One of the white captives, a girl perhaps fourteen years old, sits alone before the tipi of her captor. The braves try to make her talk, pelting her with chunks of dirt. I forbid James to go near her, but I caught him watching the men, eager to join what he thinks is a game. I hid some pemmican and two plums in my blanket and took them to her, creeping from the tipi when no one was about, but she would not speak to me. I covered her shoulders with the blanket, but she threw it aside. One morning, I will wake to find she is no longer there.

. . .

It is the ninth day of our captivity.

It is very hot at night in the tipi. I would prefer to take the children and sleep outside, but Talutah says we would not be safe. It is odious to sleep alongside my captors. The air is heavy with their smell and the sound of their breathing. They are all naked, but I sleep in my skirt. Last night, I heard Hepan and his wife. I thought at first that she was having a bad dream. She sounded like my mother and one of her guests.

This morning, Hepan said that we eat too much and that the braves will soon kill us. If they come for us, I will kill my children first, strangle them or smother them. Then I will kill myself.

. . .

The Lost Wife

Chaska came this afternoon. When I asked him where he had been, he said he'd been rounding up horses. There are hundreds of horses loose on the prairie, he said. And oxen and hogs. And women, I thought. Women and children.

He'd come to warn me that men were looking for us. He gave me a pouch of crackers and a tin cup. Talutah tied Anne to my back and James and I followed her from camp, walking for an hour in a light rain before we reached the bottom of a ravine, where she hid us in the tall grass bordering a stream. She erased our tracks with a handful of reeds and spread mud on our faces to protect us from the mosquitoes. I could hear men running along the bluff and gunshots and shouts. There was a sickening smell, perhaps a dead animal. I begged her not to leave us, but she promised to return by morning.

It was cold once the sun went down. I gave the children some of the crackers, and water in the cup. James fell asleep, his head under my arm, but Anne would not be soothed. When I held my hand to her mouth to muffle her cries, she bit me. I whispered stories to her, "Rapunzel" and "The Little Match Girl," until she fell asleep, her feet in James's hair. James had been crying in his sleep and looked around in confusion. He asked why the men wished to kill us, and I said I did not know as we had always been their friends. He asked me to take him home and put him in his bed, as his father would not like him to stay out all night, and I said that I would. When I begged him to be still, he said, "Yes, I have been dreaming."

There was a storm near morning with flashes of heat lightning. Mud poured down the side of the ravine. There was the cold smell of wet earth and the sound of small scuffling feet, urgent and furtive. I begged the Lord to spare us, and my husband, and Henrietta, and the men and women and children at the agency, and the Dakota who did not wish to fight. I, who have never begged for anything. I said the prayers to the Blessed Virgin which the madwomen at Dexter repeated for nine days in the hope of earning a shorter sentence in Purgatory. "Mary, graceful mother, help me, take my hand, a long farewell to yesternight."

The rain at last stopped. The bank was marked with the tracks of small animals. Mist rose from the stream, and drops of moisture glistened on the reeds. A sinuous white band hovered over the water. There were pools in the rocks and silver minnows in the shallows. I gave the children what was left of the crackers, sodden with rain, and some water. Our faces were swollen with bites. As I knelt on the bank to drink, breathing the smell of the mud, I saw my reflection. My hair had come loose and was matted around my ears. I looked like one of the crazy women at Dexter.

It soon grew warm, and I made hats for the children with leaves. There were streaks of blood on their faces where they had been bitten by mosquitoes. There was a copse of serviceberries farther downstream, and we sat on the bank and ate the fruit while our clothes dried. I had given up hope that Talutah would return. Our only choice was to walk east once it was dark. As I was washing the blood and berry juice from their faces, I saw Talutah wading in the shallows. I ran upstream, dragging the children behind me through the water and fell into her arms, weeping with relief. She carried the children up the muddy bank one at a time, leaving them hidden in the grass when she returned to pull me from the stream.

The Lost Wife

I followed her through the woods, stopping now and then to rest until we at last reached an empty lodge. We covered the children with rugs and I sat close to the fire. Talutah left to fetch berries for tea and returned with her shawl full of plums. When we had eaten all that she had brought, we continued on our way.

It was near dusk and difficult to see the path, and there were snakes. James had lost his moccasins and his feet began to bleed, but he said nothing, walking behind me and holding on to my skirt with both hands. We at last reached the Redwood River and waded across in the dark, the cold water reviving us.

We arrived at Little Crow's camp near midnight. Wenonah was in the tipi, wearing a blue silk dress and coral earrings. A daguerreotype of Dr. Brinton taken in medical school was on the ground. When I reached for it, she threw it in the fire.

. . .

Little Crow and his braves left today to raid the farming community of Wood Lake, twenty-five miles away. I did not see Chaska and thought that he must have gone with Little Crow. Talutah told me that Little Crow will kill Chaska if he does not ride with him.

James is feverish and coughing up phlegm. I made a hammock for him from a monogrammed pillowcase I found in the camp. I bathed him with brook water and moved a fan back and forth across his face. Talutah made tea from pine bark. He only wanted her to tend him, which made me jealous. Jealous and then ashamed.

He was restless in the hammock, and slept next to her on

the ground. In the morning, her skirt was damp where he had wet himself in the night. The buffalo rug was wet, too, and she told him that if he wet himself again, she would make him eat mice. She wanted to pierce his ears, as it is considered unlucky if a boy's ears are not pierced, but I refused to let her do it. She takes little interest in Anne, for which I am grateful. Now that the child is walking, I am afraid that I will fall asleep and she will wander away from me. I found a rope of dried deer entrails and tied one end to her wrist and the other end to mine.

There are some things I have learned to do, such as holding a long strip of buffalo meat in my teeth and hacking off just enough to fill my mouth, before chewing it until it is soft enough to give to the children. I have been given my own knife so that I can do this. As I won't clean my hands as they do by taking water into my mouth and then spitting into my palms, I've been given a bowl and some soap from Mr. Gamp's trading post so I may wash in my own fashion.

I used to think that the Dakota who came to the Upper Agency to eat with us and liked to use Mrs. Brinton's linen napkins were becoming civilized, thanks to our fine example. Although my husband is—I think of him only in the present tense—without prejudice, when he refers to civilization he means a Western self-consciousness that holds itself superior. There is another kind of civilization, one that Maddie and I found in the donated books at Dexter Asylum, books about Mount Fuji and Dutch painting and Elizabethan madrigals, as well as the people who made and valued such things. The ladies who donated the books prided themselves on their generosity, even if they were only cleaning their attics. They thought of themselves as highly civilized and considered the Dexter inmates to be ignorant peasants, which of course we were for the most part, the Irish in particular. In that sense, civilization means language, and habits of cleanliness, and religious practices, and more particular things like one's fingernails and how one smells. How one speaks. Even your name. Elizabeth or Charlotte is a civilized name, as opposed to Pegeen or Olga. William is a finer name than José or Seamus. It was thanks to the books that Maddie and I learned how to behave like ladies. They did not, however, teach me to chew the children's meat for them or how to skin a porcupine. How to become a Dakota woman.

The captives of mixed descent sometimes speak to me in a friendly way, as if they know they have my sympathy. One of the women said that she did not recognize me at first, I have changed so much. Most days, I sit outside the tipi with Anne in my lap while James plays with the children. One of the older boys has raised a hawk for its feathers, and we watch him catch mice for it. There is the smell of cooked meat and wet hides and spearmint. There is a water bag on a forked pole and the children drink from it. James is a favorite in camp, in part because he shows no fear. He is allowed to wander in and out of the tipis, chatting amiably in Dakota with the old women. Although he no longer has a fever, he has diarrhea and wears a hide diaper packed with lichen and moss.

Venus hovered just above the horizon tonight, lower than last night, and for one joyous moment I knew that my husband was alive and that we would not die.

September 1862

THIS MORNING, TALUTAH WOKE me to say there was talk in camp that I would be killed and the children given to the Ojibwe as a peace offering. She made a tear at the back of the tipi, and we slipped through it and ran into the woods. She carried Anne on her back, now and then looking over her shoulder to see if James and I were still behind her, although she surely must have heard us as we stumbled along. Her handsome face was in shadow, but it seemed that she smiled when she caught sight of us. I had seen a massasauga snake and pushed a long stick before me, which did not aid our progress.

As I struggled my way through a tangle of grapevines, I saw a white woman leaning against a tree, a dead child in her arms. There were bloody gashes on her cheeks and forehead. As I turned to help her, Talutah grabbed my arm. She is crazy now, she said. You can do her no good.

I tried to break away from her, James watching in alarm, but she held tightly to my arm and dragged me behind her, James running after us. We soon reached the lodge of a Mdewakanton chief, and she pushed us inside. When she left to gather herbs, I ran back to look for the woman, but she had disappeared.

There was a fire in the lodge, making a little cavern of light, and a spinning wheel with Swedish designs of hearts and lovebirds. The dirt floor was piled with buffalo rugs, and the rush door was laden with deer hooves and bells. There was the sweet, musty smell of elder, and the hemlock's odor of mouse urine. A woman made broth for us with lumps of gray marrow floating in it.

There was also a young German woman, holding a sick baby only a few days old. I sat on the ground next to her. She said that her husband and younger sister had been killed at Hutchinson, her husband's ears and nose cut off and then his cock, and her sister impaled on a cherry tree, but I didn't believe her. Her mother had escaped with her older child, a boy two years old, and I wondered if it was her mother and child whom I had seen in the woods. She had been spared when she showed the braves where a handful of gold coins were hidden. The Dakota had forgotten about the money once they set fire to the farm, and she was returning in the morning to find the gold. She was especially grieved at the loss of her feather beds, weeping into her hands, and I realized that she was not in her right mind. I offered to hold the child, but she would not let me touch it.

. . . .

I awoke at dawn. The German woman was gone. Her dead baby lay near the fire, and I realized the woman had been telling the truth after all and that the killing was real and that I would have to admit that.

I looked about me in the half-light. Talutah was snoring lightly. Her name means bloodred. She is only a few years older than I am, her face like a moon. The little finger on her right hand is severed at the first joint. The nails on her thumb and fore-finger are longer than her other nails. To my surprise, her feet are unmarked, no calluses or bunions, the soles soft-looking and her toenails clean, unlike my own. There are scars on her legs, straight lines running from her knees to her ankles. She'd once asked if the scars on my wrists and arms were marks of mourning like her own, and I said, Yes, you might say that they are.

What is it that makes her different from me? I am puzzled by her concern for me and the children. What is it that she wants? My mind went from one thing to the next, my understanding, my reasoning shifting from minute to minute. I wondered if I was dreaming. Perhaps I only imagined the woman in the woods. That must be it. It is the strangeness of everything, the sense that it will always be like this, and that I will soon forget the life I once had. The person I once pretended to be.

That afternoon, an excited boy came to the lodge to tell us that the braves had returned to camp with many mules and horses, and whiskey and corn and pork, their faces painted black in celebration as they had killed many settlers on the farms near Henderson. They were distracted by their victory, and it was safe to return to camp.

Talutah tied Anne to a cradle board, carried by a strap across her forehead, and the boy carried James on his back. As we made our way through the woods, I saw two burial platforms supported by forked saplings, on which were laid corpses wrapped in hides. Over them were vaulted framework baskets to keep away birds and other scavengers. As we passed the scaffolds, Talutah pointed to bear tracks at the foot of the platforms.

We reached camp unseen and slipped into Chaska's tipi,

where Talutah hid me under a pile of buffalo robes. For once, Hepan's wife was not sitting at the back of the tipi, and I wondered where she might be. Talutah had yet to tend to the children when some men came in search of Chaska. I heard them ask who owned the children, and she said their parents had been killed at the Lower Agency and they belonged to her. I was afraid James would say something, as he speaks Dakota very well, but he was unusually silent. One of the men sat on the pile of robes where I was hiding, his weight on my back, and it was difficult to breathe. Talutah lured them from the tipi by telling them that Little Crow was holding a war council, and pulled me from the pile of rugs.

Near midnight, Hepan came into the tipi, a knife in his hand, demanding that I become his wife. He was drunk and shouted that he would make me his wife or he would kill me. I pretended to be asleep, but he grabbed me by both feet and began to drag me across the tipi to his mat. When I kicked him, he struck me in the face, and for a moment I could not hear or see. Chaska, who was sleeping at the side of the tipi, jumped up and knocked him to the ground. The children began to scream, and Talutah gathered them in a blanket and carried them outside.

Chaska told him that as he had no wife, he would marry me as soon as he was certain my husband was dead. He said that his dead wife was watching from the spirit world, and he would do nothing to offend her. He then spoke to me in English, saying he would not harm me, but that I must let him lie with me or Hepan would kill me. He led me to his rug and lay next to me, his arm across my breast. Hepan looked on in fury, then fell to the ground, moaning to himself as he fell asleep.

Chaska was naked. His smell was pleasant to me, different from that of a white man. His breath, sweet from the herbs he likes to chew, was on my face, his feet pressed against mine. I was relieved that he did not touch me, afraid that Hepan would wake and stab him, afraid that Wenonah would return to the tipi. Afraid that I would like it too much. As I lay there, the smell of him growing stronger as my body grew warmer and keener, I began to wonder why he did not touch me. I slid my hand down his chest, past his belly to his cock. He was hard, and I tightened my hand around him. I could feel him shudder in pleasure, and then he moved away, beyond my reach. This is what desire feels like, I thought. Now I know. This is what shame feels like. I lay there all night, near him but no longer able to touch him. I listened to his breathing, fast at first, then quiet, but he, too, did not sleep. Toward dawn, Talutah returned with the children, and he left the tipi.

In the morning, I sat on the ground outside, Anne in my lap, smoking my pipe with my legs folded to one side as I had been taught by the women, preparing myself for the day. I told myself to be patient and to accept such conditions as he would allow me, all the while knowing that he would allow me nothing. There was a metallic smell in the air, and I knew a storm was coming. I watched the ponies tethered in the field and the dogs asleep at my feet, and I wished I could be like them, waiting without judgment as animals do for all that is to come. I had put on my elk-skin shift, and my hair was in two plaits hanging on either side of my face, tied with red ribbons. In my ears were tin hoops strung with wire. My mind was oddly calm, even if my desire was like a fever. As I sat there, several of the captive white women stopped in front of the tipi. It had not taken long for the news to reach them.

"So you are Chaska's wife now," one said.

"Yes," I said. "I am Chaska's wife. My children are now Chaska's children." I knew if I said that Chaska was not my husband, word would reach Hepan and he would come after me.

They were silent for a moment, then a young woman with a German accent said, "If in the end, God willing, we are rescued, we will have shunned them and you will have been their slave. Answer me that, harlot." A woman named Mary Fletcher leaned toward me and spit in my face. I looked around, ashamed that Chaska might have seen it, but he was not there.

.   .   .

At Dexter Asylum, Maddie and I were thought to be fast girls, immodest and bold, perhaps because we talked in loud voices and cursed. We played a game in which she wore boys' clothes and lay motionless on top of me for as long as I could stand it. We were once caught by one of the schoolteachers, who, rather than scold us, asked if he could join us, which shocked us. Later, we improved the game by whispering words into each other's ear, words like quim and prick.

The ladies who donated books to the asylum regarded us with distaste when we lined up to have first choice of the books, an unnecessary precaution as there was never anyone else in line. Perhaps they thought we would fight them for *Native Birds of the Hebrides,* or fight each other. Maddie and I were girls not meant to know anything, not expected to know anything, and the ladies did not like to see us run off with their books. Just who they thought would read them if we didn't read them remains an unanswered question. They particularly disliked Maddie, as she refused to accept the condescension they offered her. Other than the occasional theft of food, we were good girls, at least in regard to men. We had a guileless bravado that was meant to keep us safe. Or so we imagined.

Wenonah shows no interest in me now that I am Chaska's wife. She is amply compensated by the contents of my trunk with which she adorns herself with great ingenuity. Hepan, too, ignores me, although he likes to give me a quick kick if no one is looking.

. . .

The women bring me the albums and magazines looted from the farms. Even a cat, said to belong to the wife of a schoolteacher, but it ran away its first night in camp.

The magazines are filled with stories and illustrations of the War, one with a drawing of Jefferson Davis and a map of the Union and Confederate states east of the Rockies. There was a letter from a Union soldier to his wife: "Dear Belle, we are to guard rebel property no more, and fugitives are no longer to be returned when they come within our lines. Thank God the American Soldier is no longer to be used as a slave catcher."

I once thought that the past was lost, if not obliterated, by those of us streaming west across the land, but it is not so. There are calendars and birthday cards and pages torn from old almanacs, and obituaries and wedding announcements cut from newspapers. Many Bibles, some in Swedish and German. My own torn copy of *David Copperfield*, my name, Sarah Browne Brinton, and the date written in the flyleaf. An envelope holding two ticket stubs to a performance of *The Merchant of Venice* at a theater in Dubuque. Tintypes of old couples and of churches, mounted on black paper. Samplers, and silhouettes of children, an oil painting of a prize bull, and patent medicine labels for torpid livers and depressed spirits. Diaries in languages I cannot read. A lithograph titled *Der Uhrmacher* of a man repairing a clock. Lithographs of Moses in the bulrushes and Robert Burns, and a pamphlet of the Mormon alphabet. I was unaware that Mormons have their own alphabet. The sheet music to "General Worth's Quick Step" and "Sweet Memories of Thee." I cannot look at the daguerreotypes of the men and women and children, their stiff, expressionless faces framed in little leather cases lined in red velvet.

.   .   .

One of the captives, a Swedish boy named Nils whose parents were killed in Hutchinson, has been adopted by the tribe. The women dressed him in buckskin and gave him a necklace of blue trade beads. He is skillful at driving cattle and moves their wagons and stock back and forth across the river. His nickname is Pa-ski because of his long blond hair. He told me that he has never been treated so well, sleeping with the horses and mules, and eating more than he was ever given at home.

. . .

Those families who have eaten their share of plundered food stand in front of the tipis of those who still have food and sing, "Coffee I want, bread I want," and they are given some. I sometimes see Waaske and Upahu, as well as other Dakota women who shared pipes with me, but they pretend not to know me. Perhaps they have been warned to stay away from the white captives.

It seems that even the Sioux are afraid of women. I have seen the small huts where they put women who are menstruating. They are given a wooden spoon and a bowl, and their female relatives bring them food and water and pads of buffalo hide lined with moss to string between their legs. I do not want to be sent to one of those huts. I don't know what I will do if I start to bleed. I wait for the warm rush of blood, but there is none. I check between my legs each morning when no one is watching.

A violent storm last night knocked down the tipi, and we crept under one of the carts to sleep with the dogs. Later when the rain stopped, I watched the old women, crouched on the ground like witches as they made their fires, their low voices humming and swelling. They do not sleep at night, smoking and gossiping and cooking, and then sleep all day. The indigent and weak among them are treated with courtesy and forbearance. Many of them live at the edge of camp, a place designated for widows and orphans and the men who only like men. They are necessary to the tribe, as they enable its members to demonstrate virtue by caring for them. The old people, knowing this, behave with temperance and fortitude. My mother would have been killed instantly.

. . .

Chaska makes me lie down when I am in the tipi, as he is afraid my shadow will be visible and one of Little Crow's men will shoot me. I try to speak to him when we are alone, but he does not want to talk to me. I notice that he talks freely with others. James, for example, chatting with him for hours. When I asked James what they talk about, he said that Chaska tells him stories. "What stories?" I asked. "Just stories," he said.

This evening, I sat outside the tipi with men and women I did not know. It is considered bad manners for couples to show affection, and I could not tell which women belonged to which men. I could see Chaska's profile in the dim light. His face was lowered and he did not look at me. I wished that I could touch him. His mouth. His scar. When Talutah saw me staring at him, she nudged me sharply, and I looked away.

A man named Akipa spoke of a buffalo hunt last winter near Lac qui Parle which had been a communal hunt, rather than a family hunt. The drifts were so deep the hunters wore snowshoes, which gave them an advantage over the buffalo. The buffalo are fast when there is no snow, he said, quickly veering to charge a rider, and horses and riders are often gored, but they are hampered when there is snow. Sometimes, said Akipa, the hunters are pressed between the stampeding buffalo and escape only by jumping from their horses and running over the backs of the buffalo.

Last winter's hunt was led by a chief named Mazomani. Chaska said that he can hold a dozen arrows in one hand and fire so quickly that the last arrow will be in flight before the first arrow has reached its mark, and with such strength that he can kill a man at sixty paces. Sometimes the hunters set fire to the prairie to force the buffalo nearer the hunting camps, but Mazomani does not hunt that way. He has cunning and speed and strength, Chaska said, but also humility. The men and women nodded then.

.   .   .

We are moving upriver to Big Stone Lake, seventy miles northwest of Yellow Medicine, to join the Sisseton and Mdewakanton chiefs who refuse to join the uprising. Little Crow is hoping to persuade them to go to war, now that he has learned that Colonel Sibley and an army of recruits have left Fort Snelling in pursuit of him. There were so many soldiers, the scouts could not count all of them.

Talutah says it had not been the intention of many of the Santee to make war against the whites, but when the four boys who murdered the settlers at Acton told the chiefs what they had done, the younger men grew excited at the thought of war. Some of the chiefs tried to calm them, but they could not deny that treaties had been broken year after year and the Dakota dishonored. The government refused to pay them their annuities in July or to give them food when their children and wives and mothers were starving.

The braves would not listen to the chiefs who argued against the war. We will die now, Little Crow finally said, so let us take the whites with us.

We will all die now, Talutah said to me.

. . .

Three thousand Dakota and two hundred captives in flight from Colonel Sibley form a procession five miles long and a mile wide, the tipis and rugs folded and loaded onto travois pulled by dogs, the looted goods of the settlers and traders stuffed onto carts and buggies and hay wagons. The air vibrates with the sounds of rattling harnesses and the braying of mules, and dogs yelping in pain as they are run over, and children screaming. The braves ride on either side of us, shouting and firing their guns as they try to keep order. Some of them wear women's bonnets, and lace shawls around their necks. Some carry flags captured at Fort Ridgely.

Chaska found me a place driving a wagon hitched to an Indian pony. The wagon was piled high with barrels of lard and molasses, and baskets of potatoes, and a feather bed. I nestled Anne between two sacks of flour held between my legs. James and Talutah sat behind me on the feather bed. The grass verges at the sides of the road were thick with dust. We looked like ghosts.

The pony was not used to pulling a wagon and was panting with thirst. As we reached the Minnesota, it plunged forward to drink, losing its footing on the slippery bank. I fell into the water, Anne in my arms, as Talutah and James jumped from the back of the wagon. Chaska suddenly appeared, sliding from Snap to pull the pony into the shallows.

This is one of the only times I've seen you smile, I said, spitting the mud from my mouth as I handed a screaming Anne to him and climbed the bank. You haven't been looking, he said, wiping the child's face.

. . .

One of the Dakota girls went into labor this evening. I was awakened by her cries as two women lifted her from the wagon in which she lay and carried her a short distance onto the prairie, tamping the grass to make a place for her. A stick was found and a hole dug for it. The girl squatted before the stick, holding the top of it and pressing her knees into the ground. The child was soon born, and one of the women cut the umbilical cord with her knife. The other woman wrapped the afterbirth in grass and placed it in the fork of a tree, high enough so that animals could not reach it. A rawhide band was wrapped several times around the girl's waist and the blood and mucus wiped away. The infant was tightly swaddled and placed on the girl's breast, and the women carried her and her baby back to their wagon.

Later, I asked James if he thought we would find his father, and he said he would rather he come to us, as he wishes to remain with Talutah.

. . .

This morning, while fording a tributary of the Redwood called Hawk Creek, many wagons became stuck in the rapids, and some were overturned. Barrels and dogs floated downstream. The women beat the floundering animals as the braves raced along the banks, their horses foaming with heat and exhaustion. I was afraid we would be crushed to death. I jumped into the river, the water rapidly rising to my waist. It was high summer and the water was low, exposing the rapids, and our wooden cart splintered into sheaves as it bounced among the rocks. Talutah put Anne on her back, and I lifted James to my shoulders, his legs around my neck, my hands on his knees so he would not strangle me.

A man on a mule watched us from the far bank. James knew him at once. His name is Paul, a Christian Mdewakanton from Reverend Riggs's mission at Hazelwood. I did not recognize him at first, as I have never seen him in buckskin and leggings. He and Dr. Brinton often hunted for fossils together. He beckoned to us, and James waved to him. When he dismounted to help us climb the bank, James asked if he could ride with him on his mule. I knew that he would be safe with Paul until we made camp, but when I said yes, he could go with Paul, he suddenly looked less sure and said, "I wish you would go, too, Mama." His thin legs bounced against the sides of the mule as they rode away, and I regretted letting him go. Talutah was angry and said I should not have let James go with Paul, but I was too tired to explain myself. Besides, I am his mother, not Talutah.

Later, Chaska told me that Paul wants me for a wife. He

has been trying for several days to find a white woman to live with him and has decided on me. Chaska said that if I wish to be Paul's wife, I should go to him, and I minded that he would give me up so easily. Give me up at all.

To my distress, I could not find James when we made camp. I walked among the wagons, but there was no sign of Paul or my son. Talutah, too, was upset and said that if anything happened to the boy, it would be my fault. I already blamed myself and did not need her threats.

It was soon dark and there was nothing to be done until morning. We slept on the ground with Anne between us, starting again at first light to look for James. No one had seen him or Paul, and we had no choice but to continue our journey, finding room on a wagon with the Dakota girl and her newborn baby.

. . .

It was easy to tell when we left the river and were approaching farmland because there were fences. Split rail and rusted barb wire and sometimes just a splintered post with a rag at the end of it, marking burned fields and barns and farmhouses. There were no animals or people. Not even birds.

As we grew near to the Upper Agency, it began to smell. I know the smell of dead animals, but this was a different smell, and I covered Anne's face with my shawl. There were bodies in the river and along the bank. Agency men and their wives and children, and the churns and saddles they took with them when they fled. I saw Major Weems's dog, and the mutilated body of

Thomas Quigley, and the head of the man whose half-sister had run away with their child. There were fewer women and children than men, and I wondered if they had been taken prisoner, or were left to wander half-mad across the plain.

I looked for my husband's body, and those of Major Weems and Henrietta and Jacob and the little girl, but I did not see them. Some of the dead had been shot in the face and some had been scalped, and it was hard to distinguish their features. Some of the corpses that had not been chewed by animals or gnawed by insects had burst open.

I stood in the grass at the side of the road and vomited. Talutah took Anne from me, and we climbed to the top of a low hill, where we sat on the ground and they ate blackberries and crackers and maple syrup. It was very hot. Chaska brought me a bag of plums, but I gave them to Anne, sucking only the pits. A blister on my foot was infected, and there was pus between my toes, brown with dust. The smell of putrefaction came from me, too. Talutah picked some leaves from the roadside and wrapped them around my toe. That is when she told me she heard my husband was dead. He was wounded while escaping from the agency and his body thrown in the river while he was still alive. I vomited again, spattering my feet with bile.

Tonight Talutah walked among the wagons to ask the women if they had seen James, but they shook their heads, their rugs held to their faces because of the smell. He has been with Paul for two days now. Chaska heard that Paul is riding at the front of the wagons and that James is with him and is safe. Still, I said, I want him with us, and Chaska nodded.

. . .

We broke camp at dawn, reaching the Upper Agency around noon. The barns and warehouse were burned to the ground. The trading posts had not been burned, but they had been ransacked of everything, including the shelves and window frames. All that remained of the outbuildings were a stone storehouse where we'd kept cheese and butter, the ice cellar, the stone troughs, and three brick chimneys. Two bodies lay on the path, black with flies. Their faces had been shot away, but I recognized one of them as Mrs. Flanagan, a rosary wrapped around her wrist.

Our house and the dispensary had been burned, the posts and bricks still smoking, with little flames erupting here and there. There were nails in the ashes, and three blackened chamber pots, and melted metal and glass which had once been lanterns and windowpanes. My mother-in-law's furniture had been broken apart and thrown about the yard. The glass bell lay shattered on the path, the Baltimore orioles a scattering of charred feathers. There was the smell of burned teeth and burned hair.

There were books in the yard, white with spilled flour, and James's hobbyhorse, the head split in two, and lengths of gauze and broken vials of medicine. I saw what looked like Dr. Brinton's medical school thesis, its pages singed and torn. He had written, he once told me, on cynanche trachealis. I thought at first he'd said "Comanche," but he only smiled and said, "No, my dear, not 'Comanche.' Laryngitis in children. You may know it as croup."

It does not seem possible that he is dead.

. . .

Many in the wagon train have continued westward, but some of us have chosen to remain here at the agency for a day or two. Talutah's sister Opa lives nearby in a Sisseton camp. Her husband, who prefers to be known by his English name, Bit Nose, found me to tell me he saw James yesterday morning. The news that James is safe, the relief and joy of it, made me feel strong. Bit Nose said there was room for us in his tipi, and we followed him there. Opa boiled some twigs to make a salve for my foot. We slept with eight dogs, and I plucked fleas from Anne's face as she pulled on my dry breasts.

Chaska came in the morning, driving a buggy I recognized as belonging to Reverend Riggs. James was on his lap. The boy was not particularly excited to see me, and when I ran to lift him from the buggy, he said, "I'm not a baby, Mother." He seemed very well, except that his ears had been pierced. The lobes were swollen, and there was a scab around the metal ring in one of his ears. When I tried to remove the earring, he howled in pain.

Later, he did not seem to mind when I sang him and Anne to sleep.

. . .

A party of warriors left this morning to track Colonel Sibley, arming and dressing themselves with a great clamor of drums and singing. The war ponies, their eyes rolling in excitement, were painted with black and red designs and decorated with strips of red cloth and feathers and bells. They wore discs of brass and silver in their ears and wreaths of green leaves. Scalps had been tied to their manes, and the cotton sleeves of women's dresses wrapped around their tails.

Many of the men wore feathers arranged horizontally in their hair as a sign they had touched an enemy slain in battle, or had killed a man or woman themselves. Two of the men wore Mrs. Brinton's silver napkin rings on cords around their necks, one engraved with a large B and the other with the word Father. Watches were fastened around their ankles. One man had a trading post padlock and chain wound around his neck. Sheaves of goldenrod and fresh leaves were tucked into their headbands and belts.

Little Crow carried a war club decorated with upholstery tacks. He wore a large silver disc called a peace medal with an engraving of President Madison on it, presented to him when he visited Washington, and an ermine skin around his shoulders, the head still attached, with blue glass beads for eyes. One of his wives packed his feathered war bonnet in his saddlebag.

I watched as Chaska painted the lower half of his face red. The ridge of his scar held more paint than the rest of his face, and it looked as if the corner of his mouth had been slashed a second time. He had difficulty tying a quilled band to his arm and asked his mother to tie it for him. As his hair is still too short to braid, he wore a strip of red-dyed horsehair on his head, fastening it with a leather strap. He draped his medicine bag around his neck and rode away, carrying a double-barreled shotgun with the bullets called traders' balls.

They returned near dawn. The war party had come upon a company of soldiers which had stopped at Birch Coulee to bury the men, women, and children they'd found dead on the plain. The Dakota, hidden in a ravine, watched as the soldiers dug a long line of graves. When they had finished, the braves killed nearly all of the men and all of the horses. It is thought that Major Weems was with the soldiers and that he'd been wounded. I could see that Chaska was both proud and ashamed.

Opa's son Chayton was one of the warriors killed at Birch Coulee, his body left in the field as it is an honor to lie dead in enemy territory. His mother will make three slashes in her thighs and below her knees, and cut her hair. His father will thrust two sharp pegs through his forearm. Chayton's pony, which followed the returning warriors to camp, was given to the man considered the bravest in the band. Opa's brother brought his mother three of the troopers' scalps to honor her son's death. As I did not want James to watch the mourning ceremonies, and I did not want to watch them either, I quickly dressed and fed the children.

Wenonah, who was scraping tissue from the scalps, grabbed me with her bloody hands as I left the tipi, crossing my two braids tightly beneath my chin, which caused me to choke. James threw himself at her, knocking her backward onto the ground. I grabbed him and Anne, and we ran into the woods.

. . .

There is a rumor that Colonel Sibley left a message for Little Crow at Birch Coulee, sealed in a cigar box and attached to a stake in the ravine, asking why the Dakota wanted a war with the whites.

Sibley, who speaks Dakota, was once married to Red Blanket Woman, the daughter of a Mdewakanton chief, before his more appropriate marriage to a white woman from Pennsylvania. He and Red Blanket Woman have a pretty daughter named Helen Hastings Sibley. I know this because he is unexpectedly kind to the girl, first arranging for her to live with a prosperous farmer and then sending her to boarding school in the East before establishing her in St. Paul, all of which enrages his wife.

·   ·   ·

It is four days since the ambush at Birch Coulee. We are moving farther up-country. Chaska has learned that Reverend Riggs and his wife and children were rescued by Christian Indians who hid them on an island in the Minnesota.

Little Crow has sent a letter to Colonel Sibley with the help of a man of mixed descent named Able McQuade. Mr. McQuade asked me to read the letter before it was sent. Little Crow wants Sibley to know that Major Weems and the traders are to blame for the war. The Dakota have stood by their treaties with the government, while year after year they were dishonored and shamed. The traders defraud them of the money they have been promised and conspire with their friends to rob them of more. They did not receive this year's annuity, and their women and children died of starvation. The trader Mr. Gamp told them they were not men. He said they could eat grass or their own dung before he would help them. Many people heard Gamp say this.

That is Little Crow's letter. As far as I know, Sibley has not answered him.

The Lost Wife

. . .

This evening, as Chaska and I approached the mission at Hazel-wood, Nils and some of the other captive white boys went mad, jumping from the wagons to break into Reverend Riggs's school, throwing desks through windows, tearing papers and books, and ringing the school bell without cease. Reverend Riggs had tried to save some of his hymnals and primers by burying them, but he did not bury them deep enough. The boys pulled dozens of books from the ground and threw them into the bonfire they'd made with chairs and tables from the mission. Then they set fire to the school and mission houses, whooping and cheering as they watched them burn to the ground. The white captives in camp later claimed that the Dakota had burned the mission, and cursed at me when I told them it was not true.

. . .

There is great turmoil in camp, as it is said that Little Crow and his warriors will soon attack the chiefs who refuse to join them in war.

Anne is sick with fever. Chaska heard that Dr. Williston's mission at Wood Lake had not been burned and took me there to look for medicine, but there was nothing, only three turnips in the garden, and I sat on the ground and ate them. The white prairie orchid is in bloom and the air smelled of vanilla.

When we returned, Talutah made a syrup for Anne from the stems of some Canadian lettuce she found growing by the river.

. . .

Sometimes when we cannot sleep, Talutah tells me the old legends. Tonight she told me the story of the lost wife. A Dakota girl ran away from a husband who mistreated her, despite his promise to be kind. Although the whole village searched for her, they could not find her. In her wandering, she met the chief of the wolves who was disguised as a man. He took her to his tipi, where he asked what food she would like to eat. She said she wanted buffalo meat, and soon two coyotes appeared with the tender shoulder of a freshly killed buffalo calf. How do you eat it? asked the wolf chief. By cutting it as I hold it in my mouth, she told him. The coyotes returned with a knife and gave it to the girl. She lived this way for a year, content and at peace, the wolves treating her with kindness. One day, the chief said her people were going on a buffalo hunt and would kill the wolves if they came upon them. He asked her to stop them. The next morning, she climbed to the top of a nearby hill and watched as the young men of her tribe rode across the plain on their ponies. She held up her hands to signal them, and when they reached her, they said, We lost a young woman a year ago—can you be that girl? She told them she was the lost wife for whom they had searched and that she lived with the wolves. She asked the braves not to harm them. They said they would return to camp to tell the others. She waited for them atop the hill and soon saw a long line of people coming toward her, warriors, then women and children. The girl's mother and father wept with happiness to see her, but she could no longer bear the smell of men and fainted. When she was herself again, she told the hunters they were to bring her the tongues and best pieces of the buffalo they killed on their hunt. They promised to do so and returned the next day, leaving a great pile of meat on the ground. The girl stood on the meat, holding a pole with a red flag, and howled like a wolf. Soon hundreds of wolves came loping across the prairie to fall upon the meat and devour it. When there was none left, the young woman returned to her people. Her husband wished to live with her again, but she would no longer be his wife.

Most nights, Talutah's stories lull me to sleep, but not tonight.

. . .

This morning, I learned that a white woman and her daughters were in a wagon nearby, and I went to see them. The woman's name is Mrs. DeCamp. Her husband was supervisor of the saw-mill at the Lower Agency. She asked if I would tell the women to dress her and her girls in Indian clothes. They had no shoes, and their skirts were filthy, caked with excrement. They were starving, and I gave them some plums and dried meat. I sat with them through the day.

Later, I found moccasins and some clothes for them, a boy's shirt and an elk-skin sacque, and I bathed the girls and dressed them. I gave Mrs. DeCamp a doeskin and my blanket. She said she had heard that my husband was dead. I said if that were so, there was no longer any reason to return to Yellow Medicine. I would live with the Dakota.

This evening, Bit Nose told me Little Crow intended to kill Mrs. DeCamp, as she had been seen dancing and singing with joy when she learned that four of Little Crow's braves had been killed at Birch Coulee, one of them Bit Nose's son. I hurried to her wagon to tell her she must escape. Taking her by the hand, I showed her a path through the woods, watching until I could no longer see them.

.   .   .

I sometimes go to the river twice a day to wash the children's clothes, as they both have diarrhea. I take the time to bathe, wading upstream where the water is clean, washing my braids with the crushed roots of soapweed yucca. I shake myself like a wet dog when I climb the bank, which makes the Dakota children laugh, and then I laugh, too. Although I often sleep in wet clothes, I have yet to fall ill. I have lost much weight, but I am stronger than I have ever been in my life.

It is sometimes difficult to climb the bank in bare feet, especially if I am carrying water, a bucket in one hand as I grab hold of the hazel bushes to pull myself to the top. Sometimes one of the men sees me struggling and helps me up the hill. As my feet were especially dirty today, I washed them in the pail, then threw out the muddy water and refilled it. Someone saw me and told the women. It seems it is considered a defilement to put one's feet in a pail. Women are not even allowed to step over a pail. I told them I had rinsed it after cleaning my feet and that I would rinse it as many times as they liked, but they said it must never be touched again. Now it is I who am uncivilized.

.   .   .

The Lost Wife

We have left the wagon train, walking with forty others to the village of the Sisseton chief Red Iron, sixteen miles away at the junction of the Minnesota and Chippewa Rivers. We are near the village of Lac qui Parle.

Chaska has ridden ahead on Snap. The pail in which I washed my feet was left on the prairie. James rides on an Indian pony hitched to a light cart by sapling poles. Talutah leads the pony, and I trot alongside. She ties Anne's cradle to the back of the cart, where she sleeps peacefully until a sudden jolt wakes her and she begins to scream. Then Talutah puts her on my back and we start again.

. . .

We are in Chief Red Iron's camp now. It is quiet, as many of the braves have left in scouting parties, and to post lookouts. The men in camp play cards, staking their blankets and even knives and spears on a card, sometimes going home in nothing but a breechcloth. They play drums and dance if they win, one foot shuffling before the other, bent at the waist, peering from side to side like a bird.

There is a young woman in camp named Red Moon who considers herself the wife of a captain at Fort Snelling. Last year, she was sent away with their four-year-old boy when the captain's wife arrived from Cincinnati. She speaks a few words of English. Her little boy, his complexion very fair, is dressed as a soldier in clothes she has made for him, complete with a red stripe down the side of his buckskin pantaloons. He is treated unkindly by the braves, and I try to keep him and his mother close to me.

. . .

We learned last night that Little Crow was defeated two days ago in a battle at Wood Lake, where Mankato, one of the Mde-wakanton chiefs, was cut down by a howitzer. The white soldiers took the scalps of dead Indians.

The chiefs will never join forces with Little Crow now. It is the end of the war. Sisseton scouts dressed in white and holding white flags have been sent to Colonel Sibley in the hope of making peace. Ditches have been dug around the camp and more scouts posted across the prairie and in the woods.

Tonight when Little Crow and his men reached camp, two hundred Sisseton braves lined the path to warn them not to enter their village. Chief Red Iron wore a French officer's uniform given to his grandfather, with canvas gaiters and a white fur hat. Shots were fired in anger by Little Crow's braves, but no one was injured. Little Crow rode off with his men, some of whom had been wounded at Wood Lake.

. . .

It has been thirty-six hours since the last peace message was delivered to Colonel Sibley. No one understands what is taking him so long to reach us. Chaska says that a horse-drawn wagon can make the trip from Fort Ridgely to Lac qui Parle in three days. Instead, it has taken Sibley and his army of five hundred men fifty hours to travel twenty-five miles. They spend hours digging entrenchments and roasting buffalo steaks when they should be riding in pursuit of Little Crow and his men. Some of the Friendlies have chosen to assist Sibley as scouts and interpreters after receiving his promise that those who have not joined the uprising or killed whites will not be harmed.

Little Crow sent word that before Sibley reaches us, he will return to dress all the white captives in buckskin and send them onto the plain so the soldiers will kill the very ones they have come to rescue.

· · ·

The Friendlies have their own camp west of the Chippewa River, a half mile from Red Iron's village, and have hidden some of the white captives in their tipis. I asked Chaska if I could move there with the children, but he wishes me to stay with him. The Sisseton are afraid that Sibley, despite giving his word, will arrest them, even if they have not killed whites or fought against the soldiers. Many of them are preparing to go west into the Dakotas. Chaska, too, is apprehensive and asked that I write a letter to Sibley to tell him that he and Talutah saved my life and the lives of my children. If I am killed, he said, it will be your fault.

I grabbed his knife and held it between my teeth as I have seen the braves do when they take an oath, and swore that I would protect him as he has protected me. He took the knife from me, touching my face with his hand, but said nothing. I wrote the letter on the back of a picture of Niagara Falls I found in Bit Nose's tipi, and a boy with a white rag around his head and another around his shoulders rode off with it.

Chaska said I must change my clothes, as the soldiers will not like to see a white woman in Indian dress, and I put on a brown wool dress I found in a trunk. I am very thin, and the dress hangs on me like a monk's robe. All the shoes have been claimed by the other captives, but I prefer to wear moccasins. I undid my braids and tied back my hair with a leather band. "It is about time," said one of the women when she saw me. "We thought you were a squaw."

Tonight, Talutah took James in her arms and begged me to leave him with her when the soldiers come. I pulled him from her and told her I would sooner die than leave my children. "You know that," I said. "And yet you torment me to give him to you." She pretended not to hear me.

"You are smothering me, Mama," James said when I put him down, but I will not let him out of my sight until we are free. I removed the ornaments from his ears, as they have at last healed.

I had promised myself that I would never tell another lie as long as the children and I are spared, but last night I broke my vow. I told two white women that if Little Crow reaches us before the army, I and my children will not be harmed.

"Why is that?" one of them asked, rolling her eyes.

"Chaska's wife gets special treatment," said the other.

"My children and I have Indian blood," I said. "Some years ago, my grandfather married a Lakota woman in Laramie and took her with him when he returned to the East." I could see they didn't believe me, so I had broken my promise for nothing.

The Lost Wife

. . .

We waited all day for Colonel Sibley, but he did not come. He is only twenty miles away, moving even more slowly than before, sometimes only eight miles a day. He is said to be idling near Hazelwood, where two days ago he held a grand dress parade to the astonishment of the Dakota scouts. Little Crow is said to be camped near Lac qui Parle, fifteen miles away, and moving toward us with haste.

There are only fifty tipis in camp now, many of the Santee fleeing west as the army grows near. The medicine men have been busy conjuring in an attempt to learn Sibley's plans once he arrives, banging their mystery drums and singing through the night. Some of the captives say that Sibley is dragging a cannon and two howitzers behind him, which explains why he is taking so long, not that he is a coward.

Word came this morning that Little Crow and his army have crossed the Chippewa River and are fleeing north to Canada. Chief Wabasha of the Mdewakanton tribe sent a message to Colonel Sibley, letting him know that the captives are safe and that Little Crow has gone. There is great relief in camp.

. . .

Last night, I told Chaska that I had something to tell him—not that I am part Sioux, he knew that was a lie, but something I want him to know in case my children and I are killed.

He was braiding rope and only nodded his head. When I

began to cry, he said that we would not be killed, as another letter had been carried to Sibley that morning, again offering to return the captives. You will soon be free, he said.

I asked him to listen to me. "I have two husbands," I said, "one of them far away. There is a child, a girl who is ten years old now. Her name is Florence. She was lame in one foot when she was born, but that is not why I ran away. Sometimes I hear her voice in my sleep."

He looked at me then, not in disapproval, but in surprise. It is a sign of distinction when a Dakota man has more than one wife, as it means he can feed her and any children they might have, but it is not possible for a woman to have more than one husband. He asked if my doctor husband knew this, and I said he did not know. I said that if he knew, I might lose my other children, and if that happened, I would not be able to live.

He looked at me for a long time, but said nothing. It was as if his ill-fortune had at last spent itself and he had nothing more to give. I reached to take his hand, and for once he let me touch him.

. . .

We at last saw them coming. It was very hot, and the dust and noise were great. Nearly one hundred white captives and many of mixed descent gathered at the edge of camp. Some held sticks with white rags attached to them. One man wore a torn American flag over his shoulders. A group of girls was singing hymns, and others had fallen to their knees in prayer. Some of the women were sobbing and laughing all at once. Many were nearly naked. Others had gone mad and stared solemnly at the sky. Those who had been wounded wore dirty bandages around their heads and limbs, and splints made of withered branches. The children were pressed to the sides of the women, dazed with heat. There were a few Dakota in the crowd, silent and wary. For once, even the dogs were quiet, lying in the dirt, trembling in anticipation.

I took the children and stood with the others. Anne was in my arms and James stood quietly at my side, dressed in a white child's clothes too big for him. Talutah had made new moccasins for him decorated with quills in the shape of a rabbit and had torn her shawl in two so I would have a covering for Anne. Chaska was behind me. I felt relief, but I was frightened, too, not that I thought we would be harmed, but because I no longer knew where I belonged, no longer knew who I might be.

They stopped fifty yards away in a field between the river and the camp. The cannon and howitzers were moved into range, and soldiers set pickets. I was surprised to see Reverend Riggs among them, riding a mule. I thought I saw Mr. Renville, the schoolteacher from the Upper Agency, riding with the army scouts. Some of the Friendlies had tied white cloths to sticks and walked cautiously across the field to the soldiers.

Six officers on horseback trotted toward us. With them on Indian ponies were three white children, a young girl whose feet were wrapped in rags and two boys. One of the Sisseton chiefs helped the children dismount and set out with them for the Friendlies' camp, the girl on his back as she could not walk. The soldiers must have come upon them as they made their way west.

Suddenly, several women broke from the circle, screaming and pushing as they ran toward the officers, grabbing their stirrups and ankles as they tried to pull them from their horses, the dogs nipping at the women's legs. Behind me, the Dakota women silently disappeared into the tipis with their children. The white women threw themselves at the riders, pressing against the flanks of their horses until the men struck at them with their crops. Reverend Riggs rode forward to see what he could do, which was not much, as he was soon knocked from his mule and lost his hat. Soldiers grabbed the women, dragging them into the shade of a wagon, where they were restrained, some of them by force. The rest of us watched in silence, too exhausted, too injured to be frightened or even surprised. I saw Red Moon and her son in the crowd and beckoned to her to stand with me, but she did not see me.

One of the officers, his jacket torn, stepped forward to tell us that Colonel Sibley would come at three o'clock to speak to the captives. "There will be a court of inquiry," he shouted, "and all of you will have your chance. For now, you are to remain in camp until quarters are assigned."

Slowly the crowd fell away, and we sat in front of the tipis. It was exceedingly hot, too hot to smoke a pipe, and I busied myself with the children. It was two o'clock, and then half past two, and then it was time.

Regimental flags flew before a large open tent. A long table was placed in front of the tent with sheaves of paper and tin pots and packets of powdered ink. Two troopers stood at either end of the table. Several officers in fringed yellow chamois gloves sat in canvas folding chairs behind the table. A bugle boy came from the tent to announce the arrival of Colonel Sibley. The colonel wore a plumed hat, well-polished jack boots with silver spurs, and a blue silk sash. An officer jumped to his feet to hold a chair for him, and he dropped into it, his large nose shiny with sweat. Reverend Riggs stood behind him, his damp hair tamped around his ears. It seems he had not recovered his hat. One of the officers stepped forward to ask us to make orderly groups of ten. We were to be questioned one by one, and our testimony recorded. We would each be allowed to speak for five minutes. The camp, he said, is now called Camp Release. A woman fell into a fit and a stool was brought for her, but she would not stay on it and writhed on the ground, kicking dust into the air until a trooper dragged her away.

To my surprise, my name was called. I made my way to the front, holding my children by the hand. Colonel Sibley said he knew my husband and that is why he wished to begin the inquiry with me. I asked if my husband was alive, and he said he did not know but would make inquiries. His hat shaded his eyes, and I could not see his expression, which was perhaps his intention. I first met him when he was a fur trader with a Mdewakanton wife and later when he was governor of the state, but he did not remember me, and I did not remind him. He asked me to point out the man who saved me and my children. I called Chaska's name, and he stepped from the crowd to stand at my side. James smiled when he saw him and reached to embrace him, but Chaska gently pushed him away. Sibley and the officers, some of whom rose from their chairs, shook Chaska's hand and praised him and said he was a good Indian. A hero, they said.

Chaska said nothing. There was an awkward moment when no one seemed to know what to do next, until a Captain Lamont, rocking back and forth on his heels, finally said, "That is all, then," and gestured to one of the troopers standing guard. I was told to follow him to one of five tents set aside for women. I turned to speak to Chaska, but he had disappeared.

We were led to a tent near the river, the soldiers jostling to stare at us as we passed. Some of the women already in the tent had fainted and were spread across two rickety tables, where a girl fanned them with the hem of her skirt. I looked for Red Moon and her son, but I did not see them. The tents are to shelter us until we are returned to our families and friends. We may walk to the river and to the Friendlies' camp, but that is all.

October 1862

WE HAVE BEEN AT Camp Release for ten days. I cannot find Chaska or Talutah. Perhaps they are hiding with Opa. Bit Nose disappeared a few days before the arrival of now General Sibley, and I wonder if he left with Little Crow.

There are twenty of us in the tent, without bedding or provisions or clothing or medicine. I sleep on the ground next to my children, as do the other women. Many of the children are sick, and some of the women are pregnant. I have been wearing the same brown wool dress for two weeks. Each morning, the quartermasters give us only enough flour and potatoes for one day, perhaps that is why they are called quartermasters, and we take turns cooking in small braziers in front of the tent. Soldiers gather throughout the day to watch us, asking to see the white woman who married the Indian. Now and then one of them will shout at me, "What did he do to you, lady?" and the others laugh. The little knife with the elk-horn handle that Chaska gave me to cut meat was stolen, I think by one of the soldiers.

It is cold at night. Anne and James are sick with fever. I at last found Red Moon and her boy. I entrust James and Anne to her when I leave the tent to wash their clothes. I don't know why Red Moon and her son, who is named Charles after his father, are considered captives. Perhaps the Sisseton did not want them and pushed them into the crowd of prisoners. That must be what happened. They do not want the child.

This afternoon, I saw Nils walking among the tents. His hair is cut short, and he no longer wears leggings and his blue bead necklace, but is dressed like a soldier in a uniform too big for him and carries a drum. I was on my way to the river, and he said he would walk with me. As soon as we were alone, he spoke in Dakota, telling me that he and his three friends found the conditions so crude in the tent for men captives that they joined Sibley's army. His only complaint is the food. He much prefers Sisseton food to the boiled rice and sugar they are given. "Also," he said, "the Sisseton are cleaner. They wash every day. And they dig latrines at the edge of camp, with leaves to wipe your ass. The soldiers just scrape a little hole in the ground with their boots and shit where they like." I was not sure this last detail was altogether correct, but I did not dispute it with him.

. . .

Each morning, thirty more captives are called to the so-called court of inquiry to identify their abductors. The women, now that they are free, begin to change their stories, perhaps to gain the sympathy of the officers. Although many of the things they say are true, they have learned that it irritates the officers if any-one speaks well of her captors. I noticed that the officers who are meant to record their testimony only write down what they want to hear.

A missionary woman named Mrs. Higgins said that she and her two children were saved by a brave named Walking Spirit, who took them eighty miles west across the prairie. When he learned that General Sibley was at last on his way, he led them on horseback to Red Iron's village. A woman who is part Mde-wakanton saved Urania White and her baby, healing Urania's wounds and hiding them in an abandoned farmhouse. Another woman was the captive of a man with a jealous wife, sleeping with him on his rug and sharing his blanket. He did not defile her, but his wife stabbed him all the same, leaving him for dead. The captive escaped to a Friendlies' camp, where she was hidden for weeks. A fourteen-year-old German girl named Anna whose parents were killed at New Ulm was adopted by a Dakota woman named Snahna, who treated her as a daughter. When the officers asked her about the other white captives, she said that whenever she saw me in camp, I was in good spirits, having a grand time laughing and joking, and that she had refused to have anything to do with me. I knew she had grown fond of her Indian mother and was sorry to leave her. I hope she has not spoken ill of her.

Some of the women do not say a word. Others have lost their minds and can no longer tell the difference between what is real and what they imagine.

. . .

I was called to the inquiry tent for the second time this morning. They asked me to tell my story again, if I didn't mind. I repeated what I told them earlier, that I was a witness to the murder of Manse Hawkins and that it was Hepan who killed Manse, not Chaska, but they did not seem interested in this. Captain Lamont was presiding, and Reverend Riggs was there, as well as two of Sibley's adjutants. Captain Lamont confused me when he interrupted me to say, "If you have anything of a more private nature to tell, I encourage you to communicate it to Reverend Riggs." When he saw that I did not understand his meaning, he wiped the sweat from under the brim of his hat and said it again. He said that General Sibley finds it most strange that I have no complaints about my captivity.

My first thought was that he could not know that I have lied my whole life and that for once I was telling the truth. My second thought was that I despised all of them, including Reverend Riggs.

. . .

The children's fevers have lessened, thanks to soup made for them by one of the Sisseton women. This afternoon, I left them in Red Moon's care to attend a prayer meeting in the Friendlies' camp in hope of seeing Chaska and Talutah, but they were not there. Later, I told one of the soldiers I had to visit a tipi to collect some belongings I'd left behind, and to my surprise, he did not stop me.

I found Chaska and Talutah in Opa's tipi. Chaska said that two Mdewakanton men who had not joined the fighting had been arrested the day before and I told him that he and Talutah must flee. I was wrong when I persuaded him to stay, but it was because I was afraid Little Crow would kill us if he was not there to protect us. I said it was not too late and he could still escape to the west, but he said he would not leave his mother. When I said he must take her with him, he said the soldiers had taken Snap and that his mother was not strong enough to cross the prairie on foot. I said she had been strong enough to run through the woods for weeks on end, carrying Anne on her back and dragging James and me behind her, but he said she no longer wished to run. He said I had tired her.

. . .

Chaska has been arrested for the murder of Manse Hawkins.

I ran to the officers' tent when I heard, pushing my way through a crowd of women celebrating the arrests of their captors, where I found Captain Lamont issuing orders. When I told him he had made a mistake detaining Chaska, he said, "No, we have seven of the black devils already, and tomorrow night they'll hang. Your good friend Chaska will swing with the rest."

I grabbed him by the arm and said that if Chaska was hanged, I would kill him.

He looked at me in contempt and I realized I had made a great blunder. I laughed and said of course he would first have to teach me to shoot, as I did not know how to use a gun. "I am afraid of guns," I said, "even when they are not loaded." He did not trouble to answer me, only nodded to one of his staff, who took me roughly by the arm and pushed me from the tent.

I was half-mad with grief and fear. I ran through the camp looking for Chaska, but I could not find him. When I at last returned to the women's tent, the white women stared at me in satisfaction. Only Red Moon understood, putting her hand on my shoulder to comfort me.

The following day a commission of five men was established to determine the sentences of those accused, with the intention of executing those found guilty.

.   .   .

Several white women and I were again called to the inquiry tent. Chaska was there when I arrived, but I was not allowed to speak to him. An officer stood to inform us that a Lieutenant Tillman had been appointed to defend the prisoners.

Many of the men did not deny that they had attacked and killed whites. They said they were at war with an enemy who had cheated and starved them, and would always cheat and starve them.

Chaska stood before General Sibley and swore on Reverend Riggs's Bible to tell the truth. He spoke in Dakota, and Reverend Riggs, who served as translator, asked him why he did not speak in English, as it would better serve him, but Chaska shook his head. He said it was true he had been present when Manse Hawkins was shot by Hepan, but he had not killed Manse and had prevented Hepan from killing me and the children. When asked where Hepan could be found, Chaska said that he and his wife had escaped into Canada with Little Crow.

Lieutenant Tillman did not say a word. Almost nothing was written down—only the date and time of day and the names of those present. General Sibley, who speaks Dakota, was reading a newspaper in the shade and looked up when Captain Lamont coughed to get his attention. He stared at me, then at Chaska, and returned to his paper. Chaska, his arms tied with rope, was taken away. He would not look at me.

.   .   .

I'd asked Captain Lamont to send me word as soon as the verdicts were announced, and this morning a soldier came to tell me the sentencing had begun. I ran to the inquiry tent, but many people were already there and I could not get to the front. The prisoners were not present. I could just make out Captain Lamont's voice as he announced the decisions of the court.

Three hundred men have been found guilty and are sentenced to death. Chaska is convicted of the killing of Manse Hawkins. I was not sure I heard the verdict correctly, and I asked a trooper standing next to me. He laughed and put both hands to his throat, and I fell to the ground.

.   .   .

I have not been in my right mind since that day. It was then that I began to say things. I said it was true that I was Chaska's wife. I said that my husband was dead. I was no longer the doctor's wife, but an outcast with two small children. I wished to remain with the Dakota.

The women laughed at me. One of them claimed she had

watched as Chaska killed her mother and father with a hatchet, and another, a woman from Shakopee for whom he once worked as a handyman and who was said to have liked to comb his hair, said that Chaska had committed the foulest of crimes upon her body. "Your poor, poor children," said another.

.   .   .

It is now a week since Chaska was sentenced to death. He is being held with twenty other men in the prisoners' tent.

We are no longer watched, and I went to the Sisseton camp to find Talutah. She began to cry when she saw me. She would not allow me in the tipi. "I have done bad things," I said, "but I have not betrayed you."

I stood there for an hour, but she would not speak to me.

.   .   .

I asked to visit the tent where Chaska was held prisoner, and to my surprise, I was given permission. As I hurried across the field, I heard singing: "Jesus Christ, Thy loving kindness boundlessly Thou givest me."

There were twenty-one men in the tent, all shackled at their feet. Reverend Riggs was attempting to teach them a hymn. One of the prisoners began to sing in Dakota, "Well, a wolf I considered myself, I have eaten nothing and I can scarcely stand." Reverend Riggs pretended not to hear him and sang louder. His black frock coat made him look like the Angel of Death, which I suppose he is. The prisoner continued to sing and others joined him while Reverend Riggs shouted over them. Finally, one of the soldiers, his hands clapped over his ears, yelled at them to shut up.

I was not allowed closer to Chaska than the length of a man's body, measured by a soldier with both arms outstretched. Two men with rifles stood on either side of me. One of them nudged me and said, "Here is your dusky paramour."

It was the same face, grave and familiar, but he had changed. He had trusted me, he said, and acted out of affection, not hope of ransom or favor. He'd sold his gun to buy food for us and slept without a blanket so that James and Anne would not be cold. He said I was his wife to protect me from Hepan. He kept Little Crow from killing us by reminding him that my husband had saved the chief's life, that I had given the Dakota food when the annuities did not arrive and looked after the women and children.

I am alone now, I said when he fell silent. My husband is dead. If he was alive, he would have come for us. The whites think I am an Indian's whore, and the Dakota say I have betrayed them. I have not been able to protect you as you protected us. I told you not to run away. I thought General Sibley could be trusted. All I want now, I said, is your forgiveness.

When I reached to touch him, one of the soldiers grabbed my arm. "Enough is enough, lady," he said. I asked him if I could shake Chaska's hand, and he said I could, provided it was only his hand, and both soldiers laughed. We shook hands then, and he nodded his head as if things were at last settled between us.

I then ran to the officers' tent, where I again told them my story and swore that Chaska was innocent. Captain Lamont said I was not to get myself into another flurry, as Chaska would not be put to death, but instead would be imprisoned in Illinois for five years as an accomplice to the murder of Manse Hawkins. "I give you my word as a gentleman."

I said that I would return to the prisoners' tent to tell Chaska, but he made me promise not to speak of it, as not all the prisoners would be let off so easily. He asked me not to cause more trouble than I already had. I looked at him in surprise. "What trouble have I caused?"

"You are defending men who killed hundreds of innocent people."

"Defending one man," I said. "Not all of them are innocent."

"At least you allow me that." He smiled. "The women want to strip you naked, and the men want to watch them do it. That's trouble enough."

. . .

I dream of him without cease. How could I think he would be spared?

. . .

The tents at Camp Release were taken down this morning and the wagons packed. The Dakota prisoners were herded like animals into old Red River carts, the same trappers' carts that used to leave deep ruts in the road to Yellow Medicine. They will be taken to Fort Snelling to await execution. I looked for Chaska, but I could not find him. I saw Nils, beating his drum at the head of a company of troopers, and I saw Major Weems, riding an Indian pony, his arm in a sling.

My children and I and four white women, two of whom spoke only German, were helped into an oxcart. When I saw that nothing would be provided for us, no food or water or blankets, I jumped from the wagon to gather what food I could find, some plums and dried serviceberries and a jug of river water. I told the women to do the same, as I did not have enough to share with them, but they did not understand me, or worse, did not trust me, and only stared at me.

We are to join a wagon train of other former captives at Yellow Medicine, thirty miles away, when we would be escorted by soldiers to Fort Ridgely. It will take almost three days to reach Yellow Medicine, as the oxen can travel only ten miles a day and must be rested and fed and watered. The trooper driving the cart was jumpy and irritable as we set off. The soldiers do not believe that Little Crow is halfway to Canada, but waiting in the tall grass to scalp them, and they ride with their rifles across their laps.

We passed through scenes of great horror with burned fields where the bodies of men and women and children still lay, some without heads or arms, black with flies. There were no barns, no farmhouses, no fields of corn or wheat, only desolation and death. I covered my children's faces with my shawl and closed my eyes, not because I wished to deny the horror, but because I could not bear it.

.   .   .

We met the wagon train at Yellow Medicine, where we would stop until morning before continuing to the fort. I asked a trooper if I could spend the night with a Sisseton family whose tipi I had seen from the road. Anne was again sick with fever and a thick cough, and I knew that they would make broth for her, and that there would be a warm place for the children to sleep. The soldier said he had to ask permission from the sergeant, and when he went to find him, I took the children from the wagon and hurried to the tipi.

When we returned in the morning, the wagon train was gone. When the sergeant learned that I had chosen to sleep in a tipi rather than a soldier's tent, he said that if I liked savages so well, I had best stay with them, and had ordered the wagons to leave without us. The few soldiers left behind were told to take me to Wood Lake if I happened to change my mind, but as they remain convinced that Little Crow is waiting for them on the prairie, they decided to overtake the wagon train despite the sergeant's orders.

We passed Little Crow's village on our way. His brick house was still standing, as were some of the tipis, abandoned in such haste that they had not been taken down. It was empty of all life. The troopers wandered through Little Crow's garden and house, looking for food or something to steal, but found only some turnips and a dead cow. Everything else had already been stolen.

We joined the wagon train near Redwood, where it had stopped for the night. I kept to the back, as I did not wish to meet the sergeant.

. . .

The Lost Wife

We reached Fort Ridgely yesterday afternoon. Some of the women refused to leave the wagons. Others jumped to the ground to search through the gaping crowd for fathers and husbands and children, growing more and more frantic when they could not find them.

The surgeon at the fort, a doctor from St. Louis who had once met Dr. Brinton, took us to his quarters, where his young wife helped me to feed and bathe the children. He gave Anne medicine for her fever. Both the children were badly sunburned, and when he mixed a salve for them, I noticed that it was Dakota medicine. His wife found clean clothes for us, a dress of her own that fit me, and shoes, and little girls' dresses for Anne and James. She lay eiderdowns on the floor and we fell on them in exhaustion. I don't remember anything after that.

.   .   .

I'd heard that Major Weems was in the fort, and this morning I went to find him. He seemed surprised to see me and would not shake my hand. I asked if he knew anything of my husband. He said that yes, he was alive, and looking after the refugees and soldiers at Fort Snelling. When I began to cry, he asked how it was that I did not know, but I could not speak and only shook my head. I felt that I might fall and leaned against the wall.

He said that along with his wife and their children, John Otherday had rescued my husband from the agency the night of the killings in Acton. He hid them for a week in an abandoned wolf den on his farm before bringing them on horseback to Fort

Ridgely. He said that Henrietta and the children left two days ago for Pennsylvania.

When I asked if I could go to Fort Snelling, he said that soldiers had been sent to some of the outlying towns to keep order and to help with the rebuilding of government trading posts, and I would not be safe. When the first cart of prisoners reached New Ulm, the townspeople were waiting for them. The alarmed troopers tried to turn the carts, but it was too late. General Sibley did not order his men to hold back the crowd lest they attack the soldiers, and two of the Dakota prisoners were shot to death. A Mdewakanton man was killed with a pitchfork. A woman of mixed descent who was traveling with her husband was pulled from a cart, her child at her breast. One of the townspeople, a woman, smashed the child's head against a cartwheel until it was dead.

He said that he would send word to my husband that the children and I were at Fort Ridgely.

· · ·

Today, as I was walking to the river with the children, James let go of my hand and began to run. "There is my father," he shouted.

Dr. Brinton jumped from his horse and ran to meet the boy, lifting him in his arms. I ran toward him, my legs shaking. As I reached him, Anne began to cry, and I thrust her into his arms. I, too, was weeping and clung to him, the three of us holding him tightly.

I told him that I thought he was dead. I told him that Chaska, a Mdewakanton whom he knew at Shakopee, had saved my life and the lives of our children, not once, but many times. I said that Chaska had refused to side with Little Crow and his soldiers, and had stayed behind when Little Crow and his men escaped to make sure we would be safe. Chaska had been sentenced to death, but it was Hepan who killed Manse Hawkins, not Chaska. I could not stop talking.

He interrupted me to say that John Otherday told him we had been captured, as our bodies had not been found with Manse's body. He thought he had been sending us to safety when he asked Manse to take us to Redwood and could not forgive himself for that. He did not mention Chaska's name.

He pressed Anne to his face and kissed her. "Why is the boy wearing a dress?" he asked suddenly.

As I watched him, I realized that the rumors started by the white women had reached him. For an instant, I wanted to tell him, I do not love him, but I could not bring myself to say it.

.   .   .

To my surprise, I saw my face in a mirror for the first time in two months. I am looking very well, thinner and stronger than when I left the agency that August afternoon nine weeks ago, my sunburned skin giving me color, my hair thicker and glossier thanks to the applications of bear fat, my waist and bosom more girlish.

My husband, however, does not want to touch me or even to

stand close to me, arranging with the fort's commandant to sleep in separate quarters, while the children and I are given rooms in General Sibley's apartment, which is empty while he pursues the few Dakota left in the state. I do not mind, as I do not want him to touch me.

Like the lost wife in the Dakota myth, I find the odor of white people unpleasant. They smell like yeast and cheese and beer. Macassar oil. I will get used to it soon enough, perhaps when I teach myself to be a white person again.

My husband has decided we will go to Shakopee, where we will stay in a hotel until we find a place to live.

.   .   .

We arrived in Shakopee this morning. We have nothing, only the borrowed clothes we are wearing. My husband's brother, James, wants nothing to do with us, perhaps because he is planning to run for office in the spring.

I bought lengths of wool and linen, and had clothes made for myself and the children, and a jacket and two pairs of trousers for Dr. Brinton. I found shoes and stockings for us at Holmes's store, as well as a trunk, and toys for the children. I asked the clerk if he happened to have any kinnikinnick, and he said a trapper just the other day had asked the same thing, but he hadn't any. He hadn't seen an Indian in weeks and hoped not to see one. "More room for us now," he said.

The German tailor sewed me a nightdress and two winter dresses, not unlike the clothes I had made seven years ago when

I first arrived in Shakopee. I still have not had my monthly, but I will no longer be confined to a dark hut when it comes. That is something.

Men and women, even children, cross the street if they see me on the sidewalk. Only Mr. Spankle stopped to speak to me. He wondered if I remembered him.

"Yes, yes," I said, "of course I remember you."

He said he was sorry I'd got myself into such trouble, but he wasn't surprised.

"No, not surprising," I said.

He touched the rim of his bowler and stepped aside so he could pass without touching me. "I found me a wife," he called after me. "A widow lady from Dayton." I nodded, but I did not turn around.

I had a note from the missionary Dr. Williston, who asked if I would call on a Mrs. VanEtten, whose husband and two daughters were killed on the Redwood River and who was living near town. She'd been found on the prairie by some Mdewakanton men and hidden in camp until they could give her to Sibley's soldiers. I went to see her today. It is growing cold at night, and I brought her a blanket and stockings and a wool shawl. She was sitting in a half-burned rocker without arms or rungs, set in the yard so she can watch the road. She is waiting for her girls and her husband. The fields around her are burned, but church members from town bring her food and have planted a small vegetable garden near the site of what was once a barn. The first floor of the house is brick and the foundation remains. A tarp covers a corner of the ruin, and there is a hearth with a kettle, a jug of water, and a tin of tea. There are several shredded baskets in the yard and some overturned barrels. It looked as if animals had been at them, perhaps foxes or wolves. I told her I would return in a day or two, but she did not hear me.

. . .

It feels strange to be wearing shoes and my feet are sore. James refuses to wear his shoes.

Tonight Dr. Brinton said we are moving to the town of Red Wing, a small town on the Mississippi sixty miles southeast of Shakopee, where we will be strangers and excite less attention. He no longer avoids touching me or standing close to me, but it has nothing to do with affection or even pity. It is simply a question of good manners. He is, after all, civilized.

. . .

A letter written to General Sibley by General Pope, the man who led the Union Army to defeat at Manassas, was published in one of the St. Paul newspapers this morning:

> The horrible massacres of women and children and the outrageous abuse of female prisoners, still alive, call for punishment beyond human power to inflict. There will be no peace in this region by virtue of treaties and Indian faith. It is my purpose utterly to exterminate the Sioux if I have the power to do so and even if it requires a campaign lasting the whole of next year. Destroy everything

belonging to them and force them out to the plains, unless, as I suggest, you can capture them. They are to be treated as maniacs or wild beasts, and by no means as people with whom treaties or compromises can be made.

Minnesota is offering a bounty for every Dakota scalp taken in the state.

.   .   .

For the Sioux, victory was never the point. It was their burning, unquenchable rage and the honor that revenge would bring them, their wrathful understanding that they would soon be driven from the prairie that compelled them to kill. They were always going to be driven from the prairie, bad Indians and good Indians, too, as the whites would say. But it will be easy now.

The men who were not arrested at Camp Release were ordered by General Sibley to assemble at a warehouse at Fort Snelling, where they would at last receive their annuities. At the fort, they were told to form a line apart from the women and children and to leave their rifles and knives in barrels by the door. Clerks sat at tables with paper and pens to take their names. As they disappeared inside, they were shackled and forced into carts waiting for them behind the warehouse. Sixteen hundred men, along with their women and children, are now in the stockade at Fort Snelling. None of the men have been tried. Many of them are from the Friendlies' camp, and others are men of mixed race who were themselves prisoners of the Dakota during the uprising. Many of them are dying of measles. Major Weems is in charge of the prison.

Chaska is held in a separate jail with the other condemned men. No one is allowed to see them except Reverend Hinman and Reverend Riggs. It is said that Reverend Riggs has written to President Lincoln requesting mercy for one or two of the prisoners.

.   .   .

To my surprise, as I was preparing to visit Mrs. VanEtten this morning, my husband asked to accompany me. He had borrowed a trap to take us there, which meant I did not have to walk, and we could take baskets of food and other provisions with us.

We rode past the burned fields and farmhouses in silence. It was not until we reached her farm that he spoke. He said that he was worried about an outbreak of cholera, as he had seen bodies floating in the river and dead animals, not only cattle and horses, but wild animals as well. He wished to examine the old woman.

We found her in her chair, facing the road, her withered hands in her lap and a small pool of watery shit between her feet. She was dead. He examined her briefly and said that she had died within the last day, perhaps last night. We dragged the rocker across the field, careful that she not fall out of it, and pulled it into the shade. He said that he would send the undertaker for her body. "If he will take her," he said. Otherwise, she will be thrown in the river like the others.

As he took a swig from his brown glass bottle, he said, "They say that Mary Todd Lincoln also likes her laudanum. I don't imagine you knew that, having been away and a bit out of touch."

. . .

For the past month, we have been living in Red Wing with a Mr. Jensen and his Swedish wife. Mr. Jensen is one of Dr. Brinton's fellow Masons. They are not happy to have us, but it is not my husband whom they find objectionable. I keep to the two small rooms they have given us, but James and Anne are busy children and it is not easy to contain them. James wonders what has happened to his friends, and to Chaska and Talutah.

There is a print in the Jensens' parlor called *Practical Amalgamation: The Wedding*, dated 1839, which shows the marriage of a Negro man with exaggerated features and a demure white woman. Dr. Brinton had told me that the Jensens were ardent abolitionists. It is one thing to fight to free the slaves, quite another matter if a man of color marries a white woman.

At night, my husband drinks whiskey and laudanum while he adds to a list many pages long of the furniture and goods taken from the house and dispensary or burned in the fire at Yellow Medicine, and for which he seeks compensation from the government. Now and then he asks for my help. Were there two Chinese vases or three? Your winter shawl, but was there not a brown-and-white spring shawl? Ten leather-bound medical books, including *Principles of Human Physiology* and *Medical Common Sense: Applied to the Causes, Prevention and Cure of Chronic Diseases and Unhappiness in Marriage*. One microscope with three dozen glass slides. A keg of mackerel. Forty-five pounds of cheese. Fifty pounds of crackers. Two stethoscopes. Six pewter mugs, or was it eight? A mahogany crib. The otter muff and cuffs I gave you.

As I watch him cross out items and add new ones, I see that it is not only I who cause his despair. He has lost faith—in the Dakota, the whites, himself. The hint of self-mockery that I once admired is gone. Perhaps it was never there, and I only wished it to be so. It is as if he would like to tell me something or ask me a question, but can't bring himself to say it. Had we the habit of speaking intimately, I would like to ask him what he wishes to tell me. I have much to say to him if I thought he would care to listen.

He did remind me this morning that I am not the only white woman to have survived captivity. Other white women were not as obliging. They refused to dress in buckskin and moccasins and braid their hair, and did not converse happily with their captors in Dakota, yet they are now at home with their loving families, untainted by shame and dishonor. "But perhaps you liked it," he said.

December 1862

WE HAVE MOVED TO our own house. My mother-in-law promises to send us furniture and some silver. A young German girl named Dora helps me with the children. As she does not speak English, she knows nothing about me yet.

James returned from his first day at school without his shoes and with a bruise on his forehead, which the teacher said was caused by a fall from a swing, but I didn't believe her. I will keep him at home with me. Anne is talking, although in Dakota. Dr. Brinton asks that the children speak only English, but when I put them to sleep and he cannot hear me, I sing to them in Dakota. I have told him that I wish to return to the East and that I will take the children with me, but I can see that he doesn't believe me, perhaps because I seldom leave the house.

There was a letter in the newspaper today in which I am called a "Mono Maniac." It is reported that I am unstable and suffer from frequent attacks of nerves. My husband read the letter aloud at breakfast. "You are a part of history now." He then spoke Chaska's name for the first time, wondering why I have gone to such trouble to defend the man who held us captive. "I'm grateful that you and the children were spared, but I wish you'd kept your mouth shut. It's no wonder you are shunned. I would shun you myself if I could."

"What is stopping you?" I asked. "To be here is to be buried alive. If you could only imagine what it was like for us."

"I have plenty of imagination," he said.

All this time, I thought, the last thing he could bear was humiliation. It had never occurred to me. All this time, when I had watched him so closely, I knew nothing about him, and will never know anything about him. He doesn't believe that Chaska was my lover. That would require imagination, and he has none, despite his claim, and no imagination means no empathy.

"Why did you not come for us?" I asked. "I began each day with the thought that at any moment you would appear, and when days, then weeks went by and you did not come, I thought you were dead."

He was silent.

"The Mdewakanton are in your debt," I said. "They would have let us go. They had no wish to offend you."

"Not offend me. Perhaps kill me."

I rose from the table and walked to the window.

"I started out several times," he said. "Once I was only a mile from Chief Wabasha's camp when I was told you had been taken across the river. John Otherday sent me news when he could, but in the beginning they kept you hidden."

"You didn't need to know where we were," I said. "You only needed to ask them to free us. If not me, at least your children."

"I was told you were dead. The children dead. One of the Friendlies swore he saw your bodies." He stood up, knocking over his glass of whiskey. "Did you never wonder why he didn't leave you by the side of the road with Manse Hawkins? Why they didn't kill you, too?" He picked up his glass and drank what was left in it. "He wanted to keep you," he said, and walked out of the room.

I write to the prison every week, not that I believe he will be given my letters. Or read them, should he receive them.

.   .   .

Some Mdewakanton women and children passed by the house this evening, headed west, they said, when I ran out to speak to them. I asked them inside, but they would not stop. I gave them what money I had and some food. I asked if they had seen Talutah, but they said she had disappeared. One woman last saw her in an internment camp near Fort Snelling, but later heard she had died of measles.

The women are making their way to Dakota Territory. Some missionaries, among them Dr. Williston, are going with them. I followed them in the street for a little while until one of them waved me away, whether for their good or my own, I do not know. The story of Chaska and his white wife has been in many newspapers. A man came from a paper in Boston in hope of hearing my story, but I would not see him.

It is said that five hundred whites and sixty Dakota were killed in the uprising. Major Weems has publicly advocated that the Dakota be driven from the state, even if many are killed and others die from famine and exposure. He recommends that any remaining in Minnesota be confined to a few acres of reservation. Most whites think this a very good plan.

My husband may have been drunk, or perhaps he was overcome by the same restlessness and boredom that once took him to the gold fields, but tonight he said that he is thinking he will accompany the Dakota as they flee west. "Unless, of course, you beat me to it. That would be awkward."

. . .

Last week, Reverend Hinman, Chaska's teacher in Shakopee, was badly beaten and left for dead by a gang of white men who forced their way into the stockade at Fort Snelling where he was attending the prisoners.

The Dakota awaiting execution have been assigned numbers. The name Chaska appears several times in the list published in the newspaper, but it is a common name among the Santee, as it means firstborn. The name Chaskadon is also on the list. Chaskadon killed a pregnant woman and cut the fetus from her body.

I live in a daze of fear and grief.

. . .

President Lincoln has commuted the sentences of one hundred of the Dakota sentenced to death for the uprising, condemning only those found guilty of violating females or murder. I did not see Chaska's name or the number he was assigned. The name Chaskadon was among of those condemned to death. Reverend Riggs is with the prisoners in Mankato, still trying to teach them hymns.

This morning, I found the letters I'd written in a box in a

shed behind the house, torn in half but unopened. Dr. Brinton is a gentleman, after all. He would not like to think of himself as a man who reads his wife's mail.

.   .   .

It is the twenty-eighth of December. I read in the newspaper this morning that the day after Christmas, Chaska and thirty-seven Sisseton, Mdewakanton, and Wahpeton men were hanged at Mankato. Five thousand people crowded the town to see the hanging, standing on rooftops and fighting in the street for a good view, some traveling from as far as Missouri and Tennessee. As each name was called, the condemned man walked to the scaffold, some of them singing Reverend Riggs's hymn. They were allowed to wear their blankets, with white muslin hoods over their heads. Some of them held hands.

Their bodies were buried in a sandbar in the Mississippi. By morning, they had been dug up by the survivors of those who'd been killed in the uprising, and a few souvenir hunters.

.   .   .

Dr. Brinton has taken to reading aloud from the many newspapers he receives each day, newspapers from St. Paul as well as less current ones from New York and Chicago and Memphis. Today he read from *The Daily Wisconsin*. "Then came along Mr. Hawkins and Mrs. Brinton. Chaska's friend, by the name of Hepan, shot Hawkins. Chaska tried to fire on his friend to stop him from killing Mrs. Brinton and the children, but his gun misfired, and he had to wrestle his friend to the ground. Now Chaska dies while Mrs. Brinton lives."

The writer, who happened to be Reverend Riggs, seems to suggest that it is I who should be dead along with Chaska, a thought that has occurred to me more than once.

.   .   .

My husband came downstairs tonight to tell me that Lincoln has freed the slaves. I had not seen him smile in a long time. He is going to volunteer as a surgeon in the Union Army if they will have him. There is talk that they will soon accept any man over the age of thirty-five. He said that all he needs is a saw, a bag of tourniquets, and a dozen tweezers.

I told him that I was leaving in a few days' time and that I was taking the children with me. I did not tell him that I have written to a lawyer in Providence inquiring as to the penalty for bigamy. There was a law passed by Lincoln last summer, I know, but that was for Mormons with many wives. I have only three husbands.

He asked when I might return. He saw that I was surprised by his question. "There are secrets, I know," he said. "Lies. I've always known that."

"I thought you might," I said.

"I assumed you had your reasons."

"Yes."

"Are you tidying up, or running away again?"

"There is another child. A girl." I almost said, a husband,

too, but I did not want to give him too much to think about. It was what the nuns liked to call a sin of omission. A venial sin. I have been gone the seven years necessary for a decree of desertion. And Ank might be dead.

"A child?" What seemed to interest him was that it had never occurred to him. "I only ask that you not keep my own children from me." He went to his desk and returned with an envelope of money.

"I am afraid that you will take them from me," I said.

He shook his head. "You are the most trustworthy liar I know. That counts for something."

"I would never take your children from you," I said.

"What is her name?"

"Florence."

The children ran into the room to say goodnight and he took them on his lap and held them to his chest and kissed them.

As I reached to take Anne from his arms, he took hold of my hand. "I once thought that everyone who came west never went back. This myth of innocence and abundance is a kind of delirium."

"Yes, I, too, have felt it."

"And now, here you go," he said.

"Yes," I said. "Here I go."

He let go of my hand and we took the children upstairs to bed.

Author's Note

While *The Lost Wife* is a book of fiction, many of the characters in it are based on historical figures, in particular Sarah F. Wakefield and her husband, Dr. John L. Wakefield. I have changed the names of some of the characters, although not all. Sarah Wakefield's account of her abduction and that of her two young children by Mdewakanton warriors during the Sioux Uprising of 1862, *Six Weeks in the Sioux Tepees: A Narrative of Indian Captivity,* was published in 1864 in Shakopee. I have added facts that I've discovered along the way, alongside much from my imagination.

Unless otherwise indicated, the Dakota speak in their own language.